D0360719

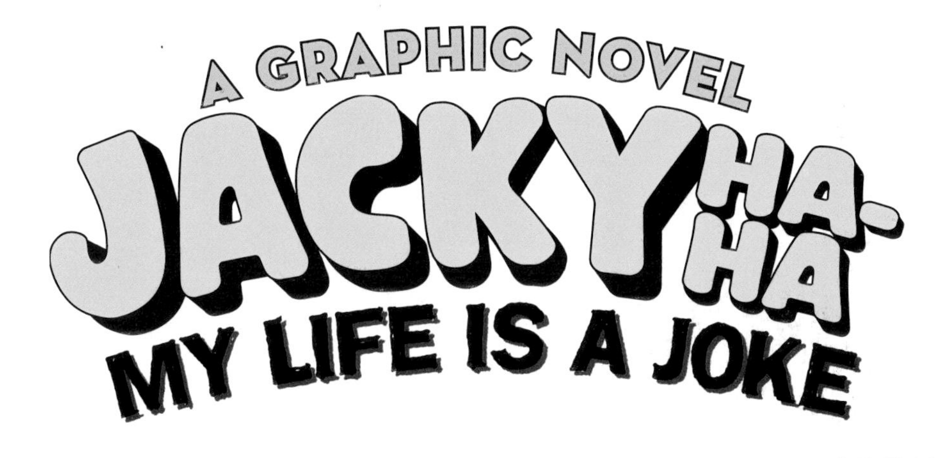
A GRAPHIC NOVEL
JACKY HA-HA
MY LIFE IS A JOKE

JAMES PATTERSON
AND CHRIS GRABENSTEIN

ADAPTED BY ADAM RAU
ILLUSTRATED BY BETTY C. TANG

COLORED BY KEVIN CZAP

JIMMY Patterson Books
LITTLE, BROWN AND COMPANY
NEW YORK BOSTON LONDON

JIMMY Patterson Books / Little, Brown and Company
Hachette Book Group
1290 Avenue of the Americas, New York, NY 10104
JamesPatterson.com

First Graphic Novel Edition: August 2021

JIMMY Patterson Books is an imprint of Little, Brown and Company, a division of Hachette Book Group, Inc. The Little, Brown name and logo are trademarks of Hachette Book Group, Inc. The JIMMY Patterson Books® name and logo are trademarks of JBP Business, LLC.

The publisher is not responsible for websites (or their content) that are not owned by the publisher.

The Hachette Speakers Bureau provides a wide range of authors for speaking events. To find out more, go to hachettespeakersbureau.com or call (866) 376-6591.

Cataloging-in-publication data has been applied for at the Library of Congress.

ISBN 978-0-316-49789-3

Printing 1, 2021

Printed in the U.S.A.

MOM
Calling...
AHHHHHH!
Hi, Mom!
Greetings from jolly old England, dear daughters and husband!
How's the play going?
She's still in rehearsal.
Oh, that's right!
Even so, my heart is racing! I haven't been this nervous since the time I climbed the Ferris wheel on the boardwalk at Seaside Heights as a kid. Playing a part in a William Sh-Sh-Shakespeare play, in London, at the re-creation of the Globe Theatre where it was first performed over four hundred years ago is nerve-wracking! Terrifying, even!

You'll be great, honey!
I'm going to do my best! I guess I'm shaky because being in this play reminds me of one of the most colossal failures in my whole life.
What are you talking about?
You may know me as an Academy Award–winning funny lady and star of *Saturday Night Live*, but...
...that's not who I used to be, especially this one summer when I was about your age.
I was a mess. And a failure.
Hey!
The star of a one-woman disaster movie.
So rude!

Story time!
Woo-hoo!
It was the summer of 1991.
Teenage Mutant Ninja Turtle toys were huge.
Everyone was saying "Hasta la vista, baby," to each other because Ah-nold Schwarzenegger said it in a movie called Terminator 2: Judgment Day.
I'll (probably) be back.
And the greatest invention in the history of inventions, the Super Nintendo Entertainment System, was distracting hordes of children across America.

In March, Mom came home from Operation Desert Shield.
HA HA HA HA!
WOOF!
It was great to have her back in charge of running the Hart house.
I want to see those dishes shine, girls!
If I can't see my reflection, they're not clean enough!
Or it means you're a vampire, Emma.
Giggle!
Yuck it up, Riley. You and Jacky are the ones who will have to redo them if they're not spotless!
COOK

Things were humming along at school, too.
Seaside Heights Middle School
Yours truly hadn't had detention since playing Snoopy in the fall musical, You're a Good Man, Charlie Brown.
Supper time!
And you know me well enough to realize that me not having detention was a miracle!
Detention
Detention

I also did the spring show, a comedy called You Can't Take It with You.
I played Essie Carmichael, a kooky candymaker who dreams of being a ballerina, even though she's a terrible dancer.
Which was a perfect part for me, since I was and always have been a terrible dancer myself!
So it was June and life was pretty sweet.
APRIL 1991
MARCH 1991
SCHOOL IS OUT!
MOM'S HOME!

RIIIINNNGG!
So, what are your big plans when school's out?
Oh, the usual.
Goofing off.
Lazing around.
Hitting the beach.
Doing a whole lot of nothing.

What about you?
Everything you said sounds pretty good to me.
Yup, this is going to be the best, laziest, most do-nothing summer ever!
Oh, good, you're here. Come and sit down. We're having a family meeting.
Girls, I have some terrific news!
We're going to Disney World?
You ask that every year, Riley.
Well, one of these times I'm going to be right, Sophia.

Ha-ha-ha! Not this summer, dear. Your father has a new job!
You're not going to manage the lifeguards?
No, Victoria. In fact, I'm taking the first steps on the road to my dream job.
You're going to be a cop? Oh, Dad, that's so wonderful! All your hard work!
All your studying!
Woo-hoo!
All your nights away from home....
Thank you, ladies. I couldn't have done it without your support.
And he won't be able to continue doing it without your support.
That's right, girls. I know school's nearly over.

And that you all had big plans for the summer.
"Had" plans?
I am now a Seasonal Class One Officer with the Seaside Heights Police Department.
And if things go well this summer, we're pretty sure your father will be offered a full-time job on the force right after Labor Day.
One seasonal officer per year is typically offered a full-time job. My days of heading up the lifeguarding crew are over, ladies!
Hoo-ah!
Eventually, the police department job will give your father a nice salary.
And benefits!

But....
There's always a but. And this sounds like a big one.
The pay stinks, and there are no benefits right now. Plus, I have to buy my own uniforms.
What about your pistol? Do you have to buy that, too?
Seasonal officers don't carry sidearms. Mostly we write tickets, reduce traffic congestion, check beach badges. That sort of thing.

And I have enrolled in an eight-week intensive summer training program at the community college, since it's my dream to also become a police officer.
So your mother will not be pulling in any money, as she won't have a salary for two months.
We won't be able to do as much cooking, cleaning, and childcare, either.
So we need your help, kids.
I think this is the part where "had" summer plans comes in.

Yes, Jacky. We need you girls to find jobs this summer. All of you who are old enough to work need to bring home a steady paycheck.
Otherwise we may not be able to afford groceries.
Gasp!
They're always hiring summer help on the boardwalk. Plus, it'll be a good experience for all of you.
And you can keep half of your pay.
But unfortunately, all allowances will forthwith be suspended until after Labor Day.
We're also going to need some help in the babysitting department.
Don't worry, I'll go easy on you guys.

What about me?
You're eleven. You'll have to look after yourself and help around the house.
And if Jacky can't find a job, she can help you.
Ha Ha Ha
Sure, go have fun. I'll just wither away here.
The next day...
It's not all bad.

At least we get to keep half.
Yeah. I guess our ride on the Mom and Dad gravy train is over.
By the way, why would anybody want to haul gravy around on a train? Wouldn't the gravy slosh over the sides of the cargo cars?
Sometimes I think your brain is broken, Jacky.
Giggle!
Aww. And sometimes you say the nicest things, Riley!
Oh, good, Jacky, you're here. They need you in the office. Now!
Am I in trouble already, Ms. O'Mara? Because it's not even eight thirty and I haven't done the thing I was going to do yet.
In fact, it's so harmless I'm sure I wouldn't get sent to the office for it—

No, no, it's nothing like that. Lauren Furtado is out sick. Mrs. Turner needs you to do the morning announcements.
Wh-what?! N-n-no way. Uh-uh.
Come on, Jacky. It's time for the understudy to go on.
B-b-but c-c-couldn't y-y-you f-f-find s-s-someone else?
You'll do fine. You're every bit as talented as Lauren Furtado.
You know me, Ms. O'Mara. This is a c-c-cold reading. I forget all the st-st-stuff you t-t-taught me about controlling my sp-sp-speech impediment when I can't prepare!
Don't worry. I'll be there to support you.
VICE PRINCIPAL
I'm not worried about getting support, Ms. O'Mara.
My st-st-stuttering tongue doesn't care about p-p-positive reinforcement!
VICE PRINC

Hey!
I'm n-n-no L-L-Lauren F-F-Furtado.
Oh, don't underestimate yourself, Jacky.
Good luck! Just take your time and be you.

Good morning, Seaside Heights Middle School!
Happy birthday to:
- Debbie Swierczynski
- Maria Mercado
- Andy Molisch
- Vicky Chen
- Angie Duran
- Sam & Emma Waggoner
Everyone be sure to wish them a happy birthday.
Swierczynski
How do you pronounce—
You're on!
Click!
GULP!

Good....mor....ning....
Sea....side....Heights....
Mid....dle....School.
H-h-happy b-b-birthday
to....to Deb-bie....S-S-Swer....
uh....Deb-bie Sw-sw-swerve....
Sw-sw-sweerz....cuz-zzzzee....
zzzin....zzzine....ska-nin-ski-
zebra-ski-slope!
Which is
to say—
Jacky Hart,
you crack me up!
You know how to
pronounce Debbie's
last name....
I do?
I mean,
yes! I do.

It's Swierczynski.
Exactly.
But you couldn't help doing a comic bit on it, could you?
This is why Ms. O'Mara was such a good friend. She decided to rescue me by improvising a scene.
And I don't stutter when I'm playing a part in a scene.
Yeah. Sorry, Debbie. I was just kicking off our school-wide celebration of National Consonants Week.
Yes, indeed.
We just wanted to alert everyone to the dangers of crowded consonants. This week, lend them a vowel if you have one to spare.
Why, thank you, Jacky, for that very informative service announcement.
Brought to you by Jacky Hart and the Ad Council. Only you can prevent forest fires!

Later...
BAM!
Oh, here we go.
"Ringworm"
"Bubblebutt"

What?
Whatever.
Um, hello, Bob.
Hey, Jacky.
I like it when you use my real name.

Cool...?
Strange. All of a sudden, he seems shy. Almost semi-human.
Weirder still: right in this moment, I don't absolutely despise him.
Maybe all that Calvin Klein cologne he wears is making me dizzy. And somehow his perma-sneer seems sort of sweet, in that bad-boy, nearly-Elvis sort of way.
Scraggly hair
Too-cool-for-school sneer
Edgy 90s attire
NIN
Or maybe it's something else....Things about boys have started to become a little...what's the right word?
Confusing? Complicated?
Yes. I am complicatedly confused.

Um, do you need something?
Yeah. Uh, first of all, hysterical birthday announcement this morning! You're really funny, Jacky.
I can't believe I used to make fun of you back in the day.
You mean last week?
Yeah. I was so stupid last week. Anyway, school's almost out—
No, it isn't. It's not even first period....
Ha! See? That was another funny joke. Seriously. You crack me up, Jacky.
How about we walk and talk, Bob?
Huh? Oh, right. Sure.

What I meant is that school is almost out for the summer. And I was sort of hoping that maybe you and me could get into some trouble together.
Y'know, pull some pranks. Punk some people.
Or maybe just go see a movie.
Hold on. Is Bubblebutt asking me out on a date?
Flowers, m'lady?
If he does, I have only two words:
Ewwww and gross!
Then again....
He is kind of cute when he's being sweet.
Well, I'm not going to have a lot of time. I have to get a job this summer.
That's cool. I guess I'd do that too, but no one will hire me. I'm not what many consider "prime employee material."

Nice chatting with you, Jacky. Good luck finding that job!
Something weird was definitely going on inside that very large head of his.
+ = wha...?
And inside mine, too!
I spent the rest of the day puzzling over this strange new Bob.
1) 18-4
2) 3y=
4x+1
Not that I talked to anybody about it.
I wouldn't even know what to say.

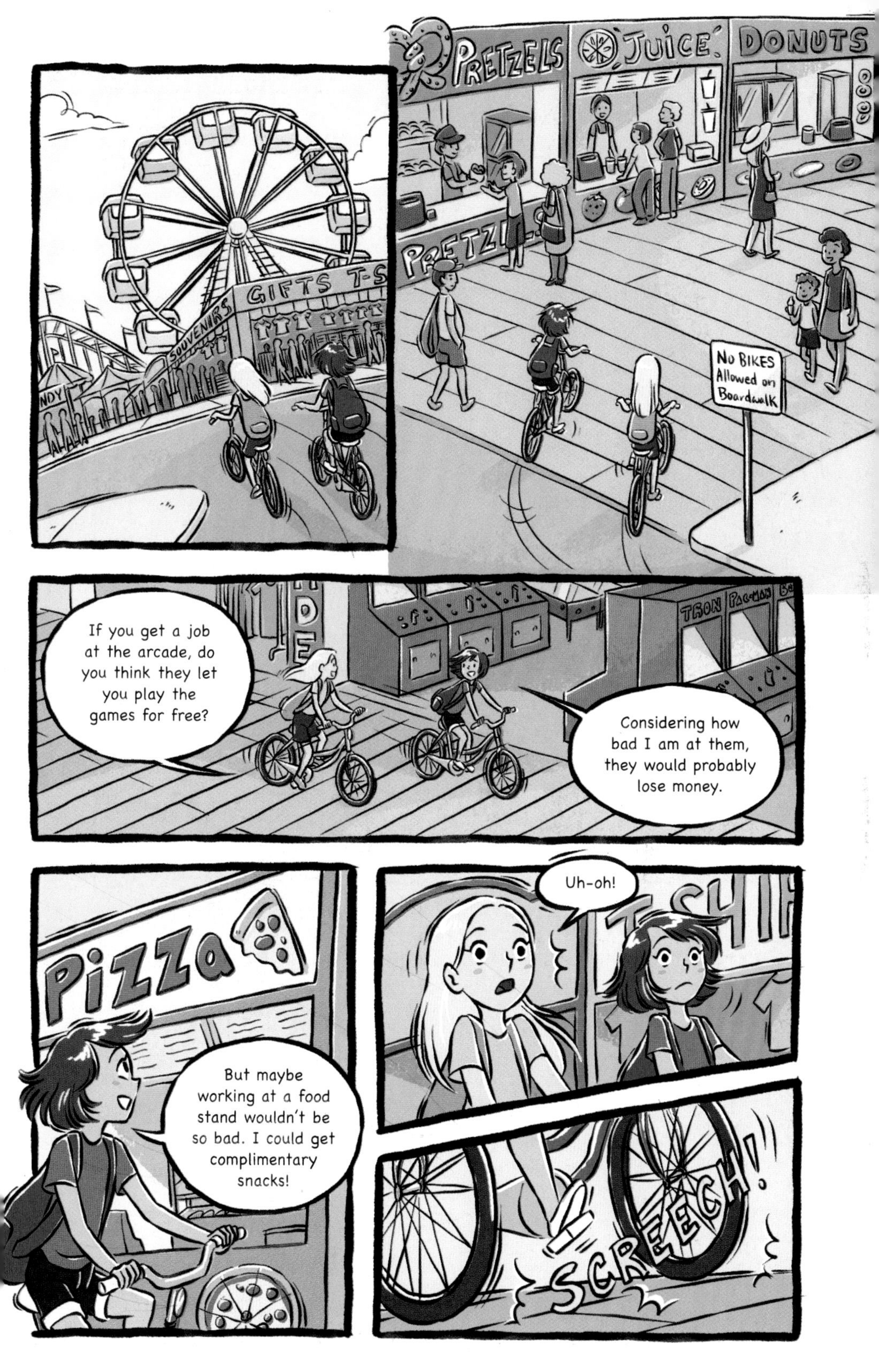
PRETZELS
JUICE
DONUTS
GIFTS T-S
SOUVENIRS
PRETZELS
NO BIKES Allowed on Boardwalk
If you get a job at the arcade, do you think they let you play the games for free?
Considering how bad I am at them, they would probably lose money.
TRON
PAC-MAN
PIZZA
But maybe working at a food stand wouldn't be so bad. I could get complimentary snacks!
Uh-oh!
SCREECH!

OT DOGS

Can't you girls read? Didn't you see that "NO BICYCLES ALLOWED" sign back there?
Yes, sir.
Blah blah blah rules blah blah blah order blah blah blah anarchy...
I wonder if he saw his haircut before he paid his barber?
I'll let you off with a warning—this time. Just don't ride your bikes on the boardwalk again.
Yes, sir.
Thank you.

I guess we better be careful.
Yeah. If Dad's superior officers find out that his daughters are juvenile delinquents, his chances of getting a full-time job offer will go down the toilet with a very loud *WHOOSH!*
Do you think Dad is going to start giving us tickets when we do something wrong at home?
Nah. That's Mom's job.
She doesn't give us tickets.
She doesn't have to. She just gives us the LOOK.
Wow. That's a pretty good impression of Mom.
It's in the DNA.

CHINESE FOOD
CORN DOG
SUB
T'S 'N MORE
RGER
1 2 3 4
ZZZZ...
BALLOON RA
Win a Tweety for your sweety. Take home a Bart for your sweetheart.
BALLOON RA
4 5 6
Nothing says "I love you" like Winnie the Pooh.
Or something.
You coming? I need to get home. It's my turn to babysit Emma.
I'll be right behind you. I've got an idea.

Excuse me.
You want to play?
Not exactly. But I would like a go at the microphone.
Huh?
Look, you don't have any customers. And you know why?
Because you kids are scared of clowns on account of that Stephen King book, am I right?
No. It's because your pitch isn't exactly pitch perfect. You've got the steak, but you forgot the sizzle.
What? You think you can do better?
Little bit.

Fine. Knock yourself out, kid. *Enjoy.*
I wanted to grab a slice of pizza anyways. I'm starving over here.
Vinnie
V
1
2
3
4
5
6
BALLOON RACE
PIZZ
But no funny stuff. I'll be right over there watching you.
Funny stuff is my forte, Vinnie. But I'm honest, if that's what you're worried about.
What, me, worry?
I felt the same rush of adrenaline I always feel right before I go on stage. It shoots up to my head, tickles my nose, and tingles my toes.

It's the best feeling in the world—I kid you not.
It's *showtime!*
Ladies and gentlemen, boys and girls, step right up! One of these clowns is about to go down. We're going to burst his bubble!
BALLOO
TOYS
SPICY
LOON R
Vinnie
$1 TO PLAY
Say, do you know what happened to the circus lion after he ate a clown? He felt funny!
I'll play!

If anybody wants to take over a clown's job, those are some big shoes to fill!
WATER BALLOON RACE
BALLOON RACE
3 4
HA HA HA
$1 TO
She's good!
Gotta say, I never noticed this booth before
Don't you think balloons are weird? It's like, "Happy Birthday. Here's a plastic bag full of my breath." They're like a whoopee cushion on a string.
Phbbt!
WATER BALLOON RACE
I'm next!

Not bad! You got talent, kid. Real talent. What's your name?
Jacky Hart.
Hey, ain't you that local kid who climbed the Ferris wheel last year?
Guilty as charged.
That was pretty wild!
I'm Vinnie. How'd you like a job this summer?
Sure! Once school is out.
Great! I pay $3.80 an hour, and you get one break halfway through the day. It ain't gonna make you a millionaire.
Unless I work about two hundred and seventy thousand hours.
Ha-ha-ha! Like I said, kid, you got talent.
POP!
We've got a winner here, folks!

RHHNNNG!!
Seaside Heights Middle School
I'm going to be working in the Balloon Race booth.
Where you shoot clowns with water pistols?
Clowns are so creepy.
I know, Dan. That's why people want to shoot them in the mouth.
I got a job in the T-shirt shop.
Bill has such cute dimples. If only he smelled like Calvin Klein.
The cologne, not the guy.
Cute
Super cute

I found a job making meatball subs and cheese fries.
That's awesome, Meredith. Cheese fries are the best fries!
Well, I'm still waiting to hear, but—fingers crossed—I think I might've landed my dream job.
What is it, Jeff?
Don't want to jinx it by talking about it. Let's just say it's dairy related.
But you're lactose intolerant.
Doesn't matter. It's the sweetest summer job on the boardwalk!

Class Rules
1. Listen!
2. Participate!
3. Ask!
The More You Practice the BETTER You Get!
Sorry I'm late. I thought you guys might've popped in a movie while you waited.
We've seen them all. You don't have very many to choose from.
Even my vast collection of Shakespeare videos?
Ewwwwww!
You guys! Shakespeare is the best!
Zzzz...
Especially when you need to take a nap. Best sleeping pill ever invented.
Lord, what fools these mortals be.
Huh?

That's Shakespeare. In fact, it's from a play I thought some of you might want to be in this summer. With a cast of professional actors from New York City, including several Broadway stars.
You'd be performing in front of a huge audience—bigger than anything we had for all our school shows combined.
But it's boring old Shakespeare, so you guys probably wouldn't be interested.
Who says we're not interested?
Yeah!
I'm totally interested!
Me too!
Broadway stars? Huge audience? You definitely have our attention!

Some old Broadway buddies of mine are starting the first-ever Shakespeare Down the Shore festival right here in Seaside Heights. They're putting a cast together now.
Why do they need kid actors?
Because their inaugural show is *A Midsummer Night's Dream*. Some of the cast needs to be youthful.
Are you going to be in it, too?
Of course! I'll play Titania, Queen of the Fairies. So I suggested we audition you guys to be my supporting cast of fairies: Puck, Peaseblossom, Cobweb, Moth, and Mustardseed.
Ahem. You want me to play a fairy?
If it helps, Jeff, don't call them fairies. Call them shrewd and knavish sprites, or merry wanderers of the night.
Oh. Okay. Cool. That's better.

Auditions are this weekend, so you have time to think about it. But it would be a blast to do a show with you guys.
You're all so good onstage.
Where are they doing the play?
On the beach, on the same stage as the music fest.
No way! That thing is huge!
And there's nothing better than doing Shakespeare outdoors under the stars. We're scheduled between the Battle of the Bands and the Southside Johnny concert.

Are the fairies funny?
Definitely. Especially Puck. He's very...puckish! You know, playful in a mischievous way.
Is that where the word puckish comes from?
Yes. We get a lot of modern sayings from Shakespeare. "Forever and a day." "Heart of gold." "In a pickle."
Wh-wh-when are those auditions a-g-g-gain?
Saturday. They're posting notices at the high school, too.
Are you okay?
Yeah. It's just that thinking about Shakespeare and all his strange words and phrases makes me worried about my words.
RIIIIINNNGGG!!

Have a great summer!
See you in the fall!
Seaside Heights Middle School

The next morning...
AHHHHH!
School is out for the summer, and I'm reporting for duty at my first day of work.
BALLOON RACE
1 2 3 4 5 6
Okay, Funny Girl. Here come the suckers. Start reeling them in.
1 2 3 4
Watch and learn, Vinnie.

1
2
3
4
BALLOON
Ladies and Gentlemen! There's nothing more satisfying than the tears of a clown when people shoot him in the face with a squirt gun!
Bozo goes bananas. It's pop-goes-the-weasel time.
Step right up, folks! Don't be shy!
SQUIRT!
POP!
Don't let their surprised expressions fool you! The clowns don't mind!
They're well hydrated.
They love what they do....
Because it's what they were made to do!

We've got a winner!
SQUIRT!
ONE
3 4 5 6
PLAY

Take a lunch break, kid. I already doubled the money from yesterday when I didn't have you.
Thanks, Vinnie!
LLOON
Italian Food
FRI
&MO
This is a good place to meet. It's practically a dead-center spot between all our jobs.
How was your morning?
Slow. Nobody really wants meatball subs and cheese fries for breakfast.
I sold five T-shirts. Three that said STUPID. Two with fingers pointing sideways that said I'M WITH STUPID.
I guess one of the "Stupids" really was.

Hey, guys.
Um, what are you doing here?
School's out and I'm on vacation. I thought I should eat some vacation food, which, by the way, is much better than cafeteria food.
I also wanted to talk to you guys about the Shakespeare show.
Borrr-ing!
Jacky, you're not giving poor Bill a chance. Don't say he's boring.
Wait. You don't think I'm boring, do you, Jacky?
Of course not! You're, you know... practical.
Isn't that just another word for boring?
You guys? I meant Bill as in William Shakespeare.

For instance, did you know that in Shakespeare's day...
...he had to make everybody in his audience happy, from the rich nobles up in the galleries to the lowly groundlings down in the pit?
What are groundlings? Are they like Gremlins or something?
Oh, I love that movie!
Groundlings were rowdy theatergoers who paid a penny to stand on the ground at the foot of the stage while the more, shall we say, sophisticated folks sat upstairs in cushioned seats.
And if Shakespeare didn't make the groundlings happy, guess what happened?
He felt terrible? That's how I feel when I tell a joke and nobody even chuckles.
I'm sure he did. But his actors had it worse. They had to dodge a barrage of rotten fruit and vegetables.
Seriously?

Yep. If Shakespeare's audience didn't like his shows, they let him know it. They voted with their produce!
Ms. O'Mara filled our lunch break with all sorts of interesting stuff about theater back in Shakespeare's day.
Like how all the girls' parts were played by boys with high-pitched voices, since girls weren't allowed to act back then.
How, since there was very little scenery, the audience had to fill in the blanks by using their imagination.
Or how there was a trapdoor in the stage floor for quick exits and entrances.
Watch out, below!

Shakespeare is starting to sound pretty cool.
Yeah. Like an old-fashioned street performer who knows how to keep their audience hooked and stop them from getting bored.
But the w-w-words. His plays are filled with w-w-words I don't r-r-recognize.
Words are just words, Jacky. You've conquered your stutter before, and you can do it again.
I really hope you guys will come to the auditions. I know Travis Wormowitz will.
Who's Travis Wormowitz?
Star of the high school drama club. I hear he was pretty funny in the high school musical, *Bye Bye Birdie*.
So far, he's the only one auditioning for the part of Puck....
Jacky should play Puck!
Definitely!

Does Puck have a lot of lines?
Not a ton, but he has some great speeches.
Thou speakest aright:
I am that merry wanderer of the night.
I jest to Oberon, and make him smile
When I a fat and bean-fed horse beguile....
M-m-merry w-w-wanderer? I d-d-don't know...
Ah'll eee ooo on aturay, mizz mamara!
Huh?

Ah'll ee ooo
aaht duh eye outs!
Mmmfff!
Hang on.
There's a hook
around back.
It's rusty.
Foomp!

Thanks!
Um, Jeff? What's with the cow costume?
I got the job!
What job?
Ladies and gentlemen, you are looking at the new Bossy D. Cow for Swirl Tip Cones!
And this is your dream job?
Of course it is! It's showbiz, Jacky. I'm on all day. People love me. I'm a star. Plus, I get free ice cream on all my breaks.
But you're lactose intolerant. Won't it give you gas?
Yeah. It does get kind of stinky inside this suit.
No kidding! Maybe we should put that headpiece back on.

No! I had a bean burrito for lunch. I'm dying in here!
Is Travis Wormowitz really auditioning?
So I've heard.
Then count me in. If a high school superstar like Travis Wormowitz is going to do Shakespeare with you guys this summer, then I want to also!
Well, I better get back to it!
Eee ou uys aturay!
If Travis Wormowitz wants to be an actor, he should really change his name. Unless all he wants to do is star in fish-bait commercials.
GYROS

BANG!
Seaside Heights News
WORLD LEADERS TO MEET FOR ECONOMIC SUMMIT
Local Theater Group to Host Broadway Stars
Are those the last of the Fruit Loops?
Yes. But there's still Co-Co Puffs.
MILK
RING!
Hello? Just a moment.
It's for you, Jacqueline. I believe it's your boyfriend. William Phillips!

Bill's not my boyfriend! He's just a friend who happens to be a boy.
I know a thing or two about L-O-V-E, Jacqueline. I've read a ton of romance novels. Did you know that the average age for a first crush is—
Hello?
Hey. Are you ready to go to that audition?
I have to babysit Emma.
Get Riley to take your slot.
I dunno...
Are you gonna let that Wormowitz guy get the part without even trying yourself?
Now you're just taunting me.
Sigh. But, fine. I'll meet you there.
And Bill?
Yeah?
Pick up some rotten produce on the way. If we don't like this guy's performance, we can give him the old-fashioned groundling treatment!

click
MILK
What?
Can I ask you for a favor?

Wormowitz is in the church basement auditioning now.
He's reading for Puck.
Puck is the best part for a kid.
And you're the best actress at Seaside Heights Middle School, Jacky.
Actually, I'm more of a comedian....
And Puck's supposed to be funny!
Shhh! We can hear his audition.

I'll follow you, I'll lead you about a round,
Through bog, through bush, through brake, through briar.
That's a lot of b-b-b-be words. And Tr-Tr-Travis is good.
Who cares? You're good, too!
Yeah. I'm going down there and I'll be even b-b-better! So let's go!

You—You're Latoya Sherron! Like, *the* Latoya Sherron!
AMND Auditions
Guilty!
You were in *Dreamgirls* and *Ain't Misbehavin'*!
Ms. O'Mara says you're amazing in both of those musicals!
Well, I always do my best.

AMND
Auditions
So, hey, are you guys here for the auditions?
Yes, ma'am.
Are you in the show?
I'm playing Hippolyta, Queen of the Amazons.
Then sign us up!
Great. Are you Kathy's kids?
Who's Kathy?
Ms. O'Mara. Her first name is Katherine.
Really? I thought it was, you know, Miz.
Ha-ha! Kathy and I were in *Annie* together, a long, long time ago.

Don't forget to write down what role you're most interested in playing. Can you sing?
A little bit.
She's being modest. Meredith is the best singer at Seaside Heights Middle School.
Wonderful! We might add some music and lyrics for the fairies....
Puck, huh? Would you be willing to play one of the smaller roles?
Well, Puck is my first choice....
I understand. It's a great part.
AMND Auditions
But from what I've been hearing, we might already have our Puck.
Travis W-W-Worm-o-w-w-witz?
Yeah. He's good. Memorized all the major monologues. Says he spent the whole week working on his audition.
M-m-memorizing m-m-monologues? I really should have read the play.

Crap. I might have blown my audition before I even started.
AMND Auditions
AMND Auditions
If we shadows have offended, Think but this, and all is mended, That you have but slumber'd here While these visions did appear.
And this weak and idle theme, No more yielding but a dream....
Click

Wow. He's pretty good.
On the outside, I was smiling. Inside, I was wondering if Bob might have been more supportive. Or encouraging.
But, you know, not as good as you'll be, Jacky!
There's no way he's better than you. Not in a million years!
Dang. I should have said that.
Wait! Why am I wondering about Bob when I should be thinking about Puck and the audition I'm totally unprepared for?

Thank you, kind sirs and madams. It would be an honor to work with each and every one of you! Parting is such sweet sorrow! Adieu! Adieu! I bid you adieu!
Why is he yammering about Mountain Dew?
Oh. Hello, kiddies.
Are you guys here to audition for some of the other fairies—the bit parts?
Because I'm pretty sure the leading role of Puck has been taken by yours truly.
High-five!

Jacky's still got a shot.
Who's Jacky?
M-m-me.
Oh, my. What a w-w-way you have with w-w-words!
Knock it off, pal! Don't make fun of Jacky.
Well excuuuuse me. I was just being puckish.
And why, pray tell, are you even here? Black people weren't allowed onstage in Shakespeare's day.
Latoya Sherron is black.
No, Ms. Sherron is a superstar. There's a difference.
Good luck in there, pip-squeaks. You're going to need it.
I just met him and I already hate him.
Ditto.

Are you okay, Meredith?
Seriously? You think I'm going to let some high school knuckle-dragging Neanderthal get under my skin? No way.
And don't let him get into your head either, Jacky.
I won't.
Hi, guys!
Travis was good, huh?
Fantastic. He'll be hard to beat.
Why didn't I at least read one Puck speech?
GULP!
Okay. Jacky Hart.
You're here for Puck?
Yes, sir.
Clap clap clap

This is the girl you told us about?
She's great.
Here are your sides.
Thank you.
Uh-oh. These aren't the same lines as Wormowitz. At least I'd be a little familiar with them if they were.
But these are all new.
I'm going to have to give a c-c-cold reading.
And that went so great the last time.

Okay. Um. Sometimes a h-h-horse I'll be, sometimes a h-h-hound.
Ah-ooooo!
That's my, uh, h-h-hound.
A h-h-hog, a h-h-headless b-b-bear...

Okay, that would be weird, right? A b-b-bear without a h-h-head? Did they have those running around in Shakespeare's day?
If so, w-w-wouldn't they just keep b-b-bumping into trees? I mean, it'd be w-w-worse than W-W-Winnie the P-P-Pooh with his h-h-head stuck in a h-h-honey jar.
By the w-w-way, what sort of name is P-P-Pooh, anyway? A stinky one, if you ask me. And h-h-how about his middle name? "The." Wh-wh-what's up with that?
Ms. Hart? Please stick to the script.

Right. M-m-my bad.
And n-n-neigh, and b-b-bark, and g-g-grunt, and roar, and b-b-burn Like h-h-horse, h-h-hound, h-h-hog, bear, fire, at every t-t-turn.
For good (or bad) measure, I tossed in a whinny, another beagle howl, a pig snort, and a bear growl.
Whinny!
Snort, Snort!
Ah-ooo!
Grrrrrrr
rrrrr...

Oooo-kaay. Let's move on to the other fairies.
Um, I've changed my mind. I don't really want a speaking role.
Here you go, Jacky.

Would you be in the chorus? Because we really want to add some musical interludes to this show.
Sure! I'd rather sing than speak, any day.
On a day like today? Me too. And I don't even really sing!
Okay. Bill, you try Cobweb. Jeff, you'll be Moth.
Dan, why don't you try Peaseblossom.
Jacky, you can read Mustardseed.
Great. Kathy is Titania, the Queen of the Fairies. She is your fearless leader.
Whenever you're ready, Kath.

I'll give thee fairies to attend on thee,
And they shall fetch thee jewels from the deep,
And sing while thou on pressed flowers dost sleep...
Peasebottom! Cobweb! Moth! Mustardseed!
Ready!
And I!
And I!
And I!
Thanks for coming in on a Saturday, kids. We'll let you know in a few days.
Great!

I can't believe I blew my chance to play Puck.
Why didn't I go to the library and check out a copy of A Midsummer Night's Dream?
GIFTS
Why did I think my stupid jokes were going to be enough to get me through?
I should've realized that Shakespeare's lines were better than mine because, hello...
$1 TO PLAY
...He's Shakespeare!
POOF!
Yo, Jacky!

WATER BALLOON RACE
Wake up, why don't you? We've got potential customers here.
2 3 4 6
$1
Vennie
Sorry, Vinnie!
Ladies and gentlemen, boys and girls: it's time to neigh and bark and grunt and oink and burn. Step right up and take your turn!
What the... What's all them animal noises got to do with squirting guns down a clown's gullet?
Vennie
Just trying to shake things up.
Well, I don't think—
Oink, oink!
nnie

I'll take a turn!
BALLOON RACE
Somehow, my goofy idea worked. I filled the line with eager squirt gunners, all of them making funny little noises.
Neigh!
Neigh!
Bark!
Roar!
Oink!
People are weird.

1 2 3 4
BALLOON

Good job, Jacky.

Here's a bonus. That animal thing worked, so keep being goofy. Goofy is good.
Vinnie
Thanks, Vinnie.

OON RACE
See you tomorrow!

JUNE 1991
How was work this week, girls?
Mr. Williams gave me a ten-cents-an-hour raise. Apparently, every time I'm working the taffy-pulling machine in the front window, business goes up ten percent.
It's because I smile. And a smile is happiness you can find right under your nose.
I was docked half a day's pay at the Fudgery. I didn't think they would deduct the cost of the free samples I sample.
COOKIES
How am I supposed to know what all the different fudge flavors taste like without tasting them?
That's okay, dear.
Sniff Sniff
COOKIE

You'll do better next week.
I did okay. Except some people just aren't very good tippers.
Including some people I thought were my friends...
People seem to like my snappy patter.
Vinnie gave me a bonus. Sales are way up.
COOKIES
Way to go, Jacky! You really found a way to put your *talents* to work.
By the way he said "talents," I knew he really meant my weird and wacky antics.
Thank you all. We're very proud of you!
Definitely. Thanks to you guys, this summer is going to be a great start to the rest of our lives.
How could this summer be a great start to the rest of *my* life?

Later.
I know in my heart I won't be playing Puck.
That my dream of being an actress is a big, fat joke.
Unless, of course, the only shows I want to do are on the boardwalk with clowns and balloons.
Travis Wormowitz, the star of the high school drama club, is going to wind up the real winner this summer.

Huh. I wonder if I should climb the Ferris wheel again to make another solemn vow.

If I ever get another shot to do what I love, I will not waste it.

'Cause I'm down for anything.
Not tonight. Besides, I made a vow that I wouldn't climb the Ferris wheel.
When'd you do that?
The last time I climbed the Ferris wheel. Getting caught was not fun.
Makes sense.
WWWSSSHHH

Hey, Bob?
Yeah?
Can I ask you a question?
Sure.
Why are you suddenly acting like a decent human being?
I just thought, you know, I'd give it a whirl. Try something different.
Well, I better bounce. Have a nice dog walk, Jacky. I'm outtie!

Sniff
Sniff

That's his Calvin Klein cologne. It's alluring, isn't it?
WOOF!

Sigh. Well, Sandfleas, we should get home.

GIGGLE

Who is Sophie with, girl? It's hard to keep up when she falls "madly, deeply in love" with every other cute boy she meets.

Shh...

So you'll be here all summer.
Yeah. I'm hanging at my aunt's crib. She's wicked dank.
Huh?
It means she's awesome.

Wow. You really are from Philly. You know all the slang we never hear around here.
Well, I'm looking forward to learning more about Seaside Heights. Seeing all the beautiful sights...
...including you.
GRRRRRRRRRRRRRR
How 'bout I go one step further, Sandfleas....
AH-WOOO-OOOOO-OOO-OOO-OOOOO-OOO-OO!!!

AH-WOO-AH-WOOO-O-O-O-O!!!!
Uh, catch you later, Olivia.
Sophia! My name is Sophia!
My bad!
Sandfleas? Is that you? Jacqueline?

I was really into him! Schuyler could be my one true love!
For this week, anyway.
Why do you have to ruin everything for everyone else, Jacky?
Yeah. I sometimes have that effect on people.
Wait!
Sometimes, even on myself.

POP!
MOO
2% Fat
MILK
100% Natural
COOK
Sorry about last night. I didn't mean to, you know, ruin your date.
I wasn't on a date last night. I was right here at home, in my room. Working on my summer reading list.
The Great Gatsby is, um, great. Especially if you like Gatsbys.

Be good, guys.
Or you'll arrest us, right?
I have to ace the course first!
Then I plan on arresting you!
Well, I better go to work.
Okay, then.

PIZZA
OBERON
About the wood go swifter than the wind,
And Helena of Athens look thou find:
All fancy-sick she is and pale of cheer,
With sighs of love, that costs the fresh blood
By some illusion see thou bring her here:
I'll charm his eyes against she do appear.
PUCK
I go, I go; look how I go,
Swifter than arrow from the Tartar's bow.
Exit
OBERON
If I ever get another chance to play Puck, I better make sure I know what all the words mean.
A Midsummer Night's Dream by William Shakespeare
What's a Tartar? Someone who invented tartar sauce?
Look it up!

Later...
WATER BALLOON RACE
Hey ho, hey ho, look how you go. Squirt the gun; make the balloon blow.
LOON RACE
I'll give it a shot.
Did Bob comb his hair to play Balloon Race?
3
4
Okay, we have one shooter. But we need two to play? Who's ready to make a clown pay?
Me.
Um, aren't you supposed to be at work, Bill?
I'm on break.
Is this big galoot bothering you?
Yes. But not in the usual way. My stomach is doing weird somersaults and I don't know why.

What's a galoot?
Look in the mirror. You'll see.
Oh, yeah?
Yeah.
Fine. Game on, Billy Boy.
Bring it, Bobbo. Bring it.
Wow. If I didn't know better, I'd say these two boys are challenging each other to a duel...
...over me!
RIIIIINNNGG!!!

SPLASH!
BAM!
WHACK!
Hey, hey, hey! That's against the rules, you two.
All's fair in love and war!
Is that more stupid Shakespeare stuff?
No! That one's from me!
POP

Yes!!!
Best two out of three?
Nah. I prefer one and done.
Whatever.
NIN
See you around, Jacky.
Yeah. Catch you later, Bob.
Here you go, kid. Play again to trade up to a prize that ain't so lame.
No, thank you.
What did that mean? Catch you later? I mean, that's Bubblebutt we're talking about, Jacky. Bubble. Butt.
His name is Bob.

So, are you and him dating or something?
Why? Are you jealous or something?
This big-spender friend of yours says he's one and done, Jacky. So you need to bid him adieu, as your pal Shakespeare says.
1
2
3
Because if you don't drum up more business, I'm not going to have enough pesos in my pocket to buy a Pepsi with my pizza.
Later.
I wonder if this is how Sophia feels on a regular basis with guys fighting over her.

BALLOON RACE

BALLOON RACE

BALLOON RACE
Later, Vinnie.
Good job today, Jacky.

Hi, Jacky.
Hi, Ms. O'Mara. Just in the neighborhood?
Yes, I was, and I thought I'd stop by with some news.
Okay.
I wanted you to know that Travis Wormowitz is going to be our Puck. He handled the language a little better.

That's fair. Travis was better prepared than me.
Yes, Jacky, he was.
Was this the big, colossal mistake I made that summer? Well, it felt like it at the time.
But no, the worst was yet to come.
We'd still love for you to be in the show.
As one of the fairies?
Yes. And we'd also like you to understudy the part of Puck.
Understudy? What's that? Do I have to crawl under Wormowitz and study math or something?
Ha-ha-ha! No, Jacky.
As the understudy, you would learn the role of Puck—all the lines, all the staging—so you'd be able to replace Travis if, for whatever reason, he couldn't go on.

You mean like if someone accidentally on purpose...
...tripped him while he was rollerblading...
What the—?
...and he went flying off the boardwalk...
BALL
DARTS
...flipped over the railing...
...and sailed down to the beach...
AAAAAAGGGHHHH!!!!

...where he knocked his noggin on a washed-up whalebone...
WHACK!
AH! OW! OOF!
...and twisted his ankle so bad...
Owie, ow, ow, ow!
...he ended up in the hospital, annoying all the nurses?
This bedpan isn't shiny enough!
Jacky?
Kidding!

It'll be a great learning experience. When you memorize words...
...I don't have as much trouble saying them.
Exactly.
Which fairy do you guys want me to play?
Jimmy's SOUVENIRS
GIFTS
Mustardseed.
That's the one who only has one line. "And I," right?
She has four other lines. "Hail," "Mustardseed," "Ready," and "What's your will?" Plus all the group lines.
It's not much, but it's what I deserve, considering I didn't prepare for the audition.
It'll give you more time to memorize the Puck speeches.
When is the first rehearsal?

Tomorrow in the church basement.
I'll see you there, Ms. O'Mara.
Good.

The next day . . .
T-SHIRT HUT
You ready for the first rehearsal?
SALE
As I'll ever be!
Sorry for saying that stuff about you being jealous.
No, I'm sorry.
RDWARE STORE
Bob is turning into a decent human being. I think we should encourage that.
Definitely. The more decent humans, the better. Does this mean we can't call him Bubblebutt anymore?
OPEN
Not if we want to be, you know, decent human beings.
What about Ringworm?
I guess that's okay for now. I don't even know his real name.
Cool.

Pals?
Pals.
SQUEEZE
We should get downstairs.
Yeah.

Hey, guys!
Hi!
Hello.
I'd like to introduce you to Oliver and Quinn Reinhardt. Shakespeare was big on twins and mistaken identities.
I play Lysander, who is in love with Hermia.
And I play Demetrius, who used to love Helena, but now loves Hermia, too.
Hermia's dad thinks Demetrius is a better match for his daughter than Lysander, so he gets the Duke of Athens to force Hermia to marry Demetrius.

Even though Hermia would much rather marry me.
And Helena still has the hots for me.
Shakespeare is more complicated than a soap opera that's been on TV since forever.
I know, right?
A lot of Shakespeare's plays start with a father trying to block his daughter's true love or passion.
Okay, is everyone here?
We're still waiting on Travis Wormowitz.

Sorry I'm late!
If we shadows have offended...
...think but this and all is mended—
—that you have but slumber'd here while those visions did appear.
And I am definitely a vision!
I can't believe I lost the part of Puck to this doofus.

Basically, it means even if you have only one line, say it as if the whole show depends on that one sentence.

And that only a small actor would complain if they thought their part was beneath them.

It was at that first rehearsal down in that musty church basement that I decided, once and for all, I wanted to be a professional performer for the rest of my life—no matter what.

But Travis Wormowitz? I think he just wanted to be a star.
The kind that throws hissy fits and ends up in gossip magazines.
click!
Usually after punching a photographer.
Celebrity Stuff
TRAVIS WORMOWITZ BOOKED FOR PAPARAZZI PUNCH
38579
I go, I go; look how I go,
Swifter than an arrow from the Tartar's bow.
Excuse me. But what is a Tartar's bow? Is that something fairies wear in their hair?

What?
I did some research on this. A Tartar's bow was a recurve bow made out of horn and other seriously hard material. So it had more power than a regular bow.
More power meant faster arrows. So Puck is basically saying he'll be really, really, really fast.
Chuckle Chuckle Chuckle
Thank you, Jacky Ha-Ha. That is what they call you at school, isn't it?

Because she's funny.
Hysterical. Tell you what, Jacky. Since your part is so teensy tiny, you can do all of my homework for me.
Jacky is doing her job like a pro. After all, she is understudying the role of Puck.
What? Why?
For the same reason I'm understudying Latoya's part. The show must go on, even if one of our leads can't.
Well, if you play her part, who plays yours?
My understudy.
It seems sort of stupid. All these people learning all these different parts. Everybody just don't get sick.
I know I won't.

Pardon you, dude.
Hmph!
Hi, Schuyler!
Schuyler? The boy Sophia was gaga over underneath the boardwalk?
Did you have fun today?
I guess.
You guys? This is my nephew, Schuyler.

'Sup.
Hey.
Just so you know, bro— I'm in high school. I don't hang out with middle school nerds.
Schuyler?
No worries. When I'm in high school I won't hang out with nerds like me either.
Just how old are you?
I'm sixteen.
Wow. You're ancient.
He's only four years older than us, Jacky.
Right. Four years. One-third of our entire lives. Do the math, Meredith.
No, thank you! School's out.
You're right. But sixteen means he's still two years younger than my big sister, Sophia.

That's cool.
You have no idea who Sophia is and why I'm talking about her, do you?
Schuyler's going to be on the tech crew.
Awesome. Have you checked out the venue yet? It's the same stage they use for the Battle of the Bands.
It's right on the beach.
Let's go have a look.
Yeah! Let's go see where we're going to be rock star fairies!
The audience usually brings beach chairs or just sits on blankets. Last summer, I actually saw the Drifters, Gary U.S. Bonds, and Southside Johnny—all right here.
I might've been wrong about you middle school nerds. You guys are okay.

Of course, the stage is conveniently located next to the boardwalk. In case, you know, you want to hang out under there with my sister again.
Huh?
Sophia. Although you called her Olivia after Sandfleas growled and chased you away.
You were the girl with the dog.
Yup. Still am.

Well, aren't I just the rankest compound of villainous smell that ever offended nostril.
You're what, now?
It's a Shakespearean insult. Aunt Kathy has been teaching me a bunch of them.
Huh. What a great insult. I need to read more Shakespeare.
So, is there anything fun to do around here?
Are you kidding? That pier over there is called Funtown Pier. Fun is right in the name!
Who's up for a stroll on the boardwalk and a quick game of Ringtoss?
It's rigged.
So is the baseball game.
And the basketball game.
They're not rigged.
You just have to know how to beat 'em.

BOOM!
The trick is to aim for a close bottle so your ring won't get knocked off course. Also, make sure it's on the same plane as the bottle tops before you fling it.
Whoa. Listen to Ms. Geometry, here.
Snap your wrist like you're throwing a Frisbee to get as much spin as possible. It's easier to land on target if the ring is hovering over it like a UFO.
TOSS
Snap!

Woo-hoo!
My girl is the bomb!
Jack-ee, Jack-ee!
I'll take my prize now.
Sorry, we're closed for inventory.
DON
What? Inventory?
Yeah. I gotta count the rings. So do me a favor, little lady. Go back to your boss's booth and ruin his day.
DON
I will. After you give me my prize.
Ugh, fine!
10% OFF!
Willy B. Williams's
Taffy Shoppe
Limit One Per Person
Now go away!

Willy B. Williams's
Taffy Shoppe

Saltwater taffy isn't actually made with salt water. So you're probably wondering how it got this misleading name, right?

When a young girl came in after the storm, hoping to buy taffy, the owner looked at his soggy merchandise and said, "I only have saltwater taffy."
The little girl didn't get the joke and bought the saltwater taffy.
The store owner thought it was a catchy name.
So, it just sort of stuck. The same way taffy sticks to your teeth....
Wow. That girl is soooo smart.
That's Victoria. She's my sister.

Really? She's so much prettier....
Boing!
If Jeff's heart had been a big red balloon, Cupid's arrow would have popped it.
POP!
Hi, Victoria, I'm Jeff, Jacky's friend. Do you guys sell Laffy Taffy?
Nice to meet you. And, no. We only sell our own taffy.
No problem. You don't need Laffy Taffy. Because I've memorized all the best jokes from the wrappers.
Giggle
Is that so?

EVERYTHING CHOCOLATE
FRESH JUICE
Where does the general put his armies?
I don't know.
In his sleevies. What are the strongest days of the week?
Saturday and Sunday. Every other day is a weekday.
What did the finger say to the thumb?
I dunno.
I'm in glove with you.
Me too!
I mean, uh, I'm in "glove" with Laffy Taffy jokes, too.

Let's go, guys. Victoria needs to take care of her other customers.
10% off Willy B. Williams Taffe Shoppe
It's true. Like Mr. Williams says, "Good service is good business."
Willy B. Williams's
Shoppe
Keep the change, sis.
I know I'll be back.

So, Jacky. Is your sister dating anybody?
Victoria? Nope. In fact, I don't think she's ever been on a date.
FROYO
CRAB C
Awesome! That means she won't have any boys to compare me to.
I know what you were doing.
I was just goofing around.
No. You were shoplifting.
ARCAD
You're right. I'm a sodden-witted lord that hath no more brain than I have in mine elbow.
Shakespeare?
Sort of. I, you know, changed it around a little.

Well, gotta go.
See you tomorrow.
Tomorrow, and tomorrow, and tomorrow, Creeps in this petty pace from day to day...
Man, I really need to read more Shakespeare.
Also, life was so much easier when I was the number one troublemaker on the boardwalk.

My babysitting shift is almost over. Riley will pick up Emma soon.
I'm not a baby. I'm six years old. Deal with it.
So I just found out that they want me to play Fairy.
Who's this fairy they want you to play?
A fairy without a name. She's just, you know, Fairy.
Well, that's great!
Nuh-uh. Fairy has a lot of lines.
Let me see your sides.
Okay. These are just like lyrics. They even rhyme, so you can kind of pretend you're singing them.
Hey, you're right. That makes it a little easier.

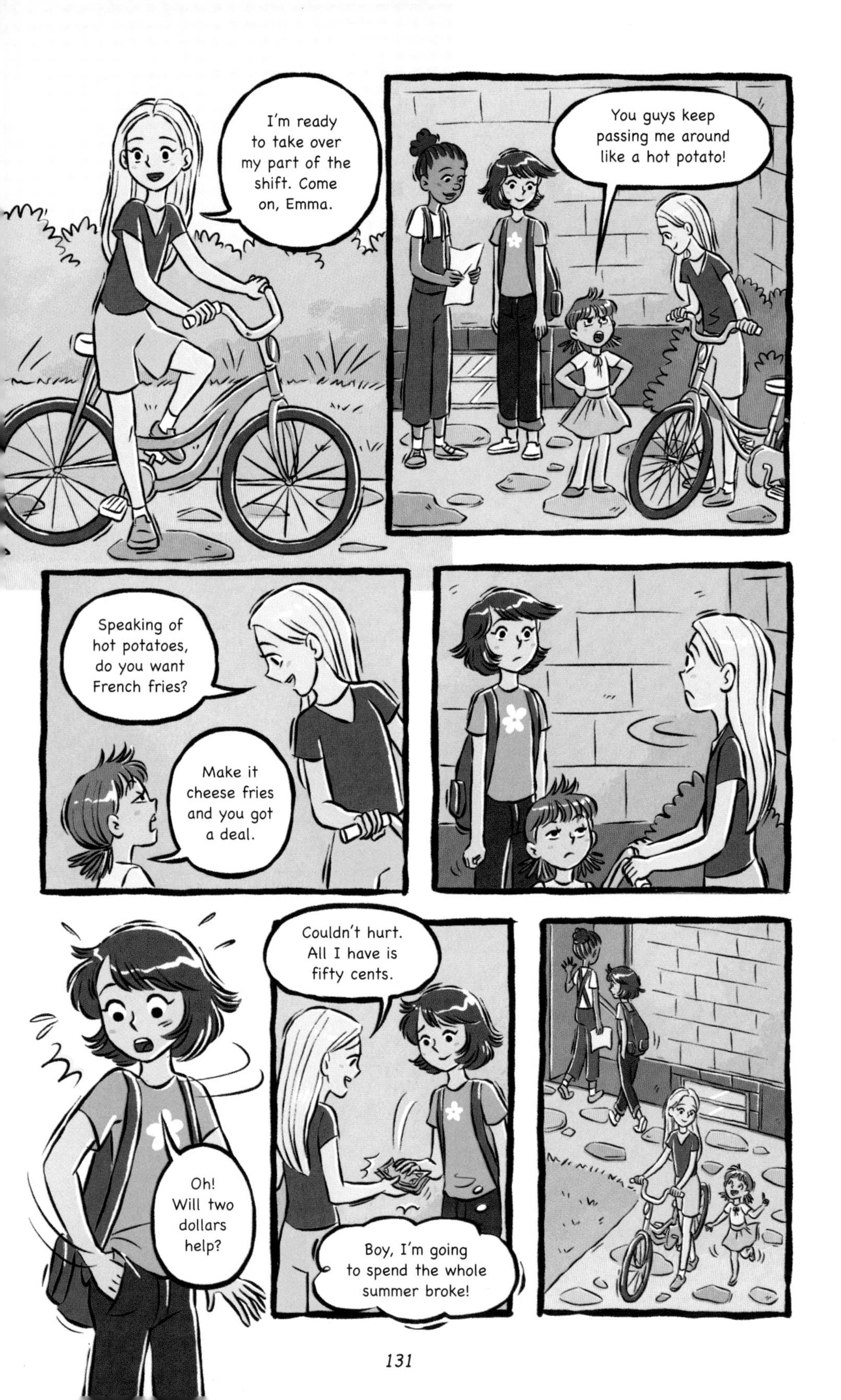
I'm ready to take over my part of the shift. Come on, Emma.
You guys keep passing me around like a hot potato!
Speaking of hot potatoes, do you want French fries?
Make it cheese fries and you got a deal.
Oh! Will two dollars help?
Couldn't hurt. All I have is fifty cents.
Boy, I'm going to spend the whole summer broke!

How now, spirit! Whither you wander?
Over hill, over dale
Through bush, through briar,
Over park, over pale
Through flood, through fire
I do wander everywhere,
Swifter than the moon's sphere;
And I serve the fairy queen,
To dew her orbs upon the green.
Cut!

Excuse me, Meredith, but this is supposed to be Shakespeare, not amateur hip-hop night at the Apollo Theater.
Do it right or go back to Harlem where you belong!
GASP!
That's it! This guy is getting socked!
What's that supposed to mean? Some of the greatest African American performers ever got their start at the Apollo Theater! Diana Ross, The Jackson 5, Aretha Franklin, and Stevie Wonder, to name a few.
Yeah! Shakespeare would've been lucky to see his plays performed there.

Travis? Let's take a walk outside.
What? You have notes? For me? I only said, like, one line and I said it absolutely perfectly!
Outside. *Now!*
Fine. Whatever.
Jacky?
Yeah?
Have you been doing your homework?

Breathe,
Jacky.
Breathe.
Yes.
Good. Because you're our new Puck.
What about Travis?
Travis won't be coming back.
Okay. Wh-wh-who's my understudy?
Nobody right now. So, Jacky? Don't mess this up.
So, my darling daughters, as you can see, not getting the part of Puck wasn't my colossal mistake that summer because, eventually, I did get it.
But hang on.
My big, embarrassing belly flop is still on its way.

When you're in a play, your cast becomes your new family.
Nobody wants to be in a family with someone who's downright mean and nasty to someone else in that family.
And you can't be nasty and stay in the family.
Unless, of course, it's your biological family. I'm sure Sophia would have loved to kick me out of the Hart family for messing up her under-the-boardwalk romance with Schuyler.
BONK!!

After Wormowitz's dramatic exit, I amazed everyone (including myself) with how well I knew the lines.
And ta-da! Since I actually knew the lines, I didn't stutter.
We should celebrate! Who wants to grab a slice?
If it's okay with you guys, I just want to head home. It's been a long, strange day.
Sure. I'll walk you home.
Maybe tomorrow.
Okay.

Don't worry, Billy Boy. Jacky's still crazy about you.
She just has a lot to think about.
True.
Like how she's going to get Riley to cover more of her babysitting slots now that she has such a major role?
Maybe next time?
Next time.
SOUVENIR
GIFTS & MORE
MUSIK EMPORIUM
SHOES
STOP

GAME
STO SHOP
FUN HOUSE
MASSA
We're Toxic Trash!
Come hear us thrash!
We're better than the Clash!
We'll give your ears rash!

Remember how Bob was making my stomach flip and feel funny?
He was doing it again. But it was a new kind of funny.
Misfit
We're Toxic Trash, and we want your vote, Seaside Heights!
Misfits
You've got mine.
Jacky? Is that you?
Misfit

Aren't we awesome?
Well, your hair sure is.
Misfit
Thanks. We're going for the whole punk look. I might dye mine pink for the show.
What show?
The Battle of the Bands! It's going to be here on the beach.
Seaside Heights
BATTLE of the BANDS
Rock the Beach!
FIRST PRIZE
$1000
The battle takes place right here on this stage. Right before your stupid Shakespeare show.
Um, our Shakespeare show isn't stupid.
Sure it is. It's Sh-Sh-Shakespeare, isn't it?

We are so going to win this thing! All we need is the entry fee and a ton of hair gel.
RAMONA
Hey, you got any money, Jacky Ha-Ha? Because we need two hundred more bucks to enter Battle of the Bands.
No...I....
Misfit
RAMON
Don't w-w-worry, Jacky. We'll pay you wh-wh-when we w-w-win. First prize is a thousand b-b-bucks.
I don't h-h-have any money.
Sure you do. You have a job. People with jobs always have money....
Whoa. Ease up, bro.
Misfit
Aw, you've gone all soft, Roberto. Just because Jacky Ha-Ha smiled at you once....
Misfit
ONA

WHOOP-WHOOP-WHOOP!
The cavalry has arrived!
Jacky? These boys friends of yours?
A-413
Not exactly.
What's the problem, Officer?
We had a noise complaint. Were you kids shouting about toxic trash and the Clash?
So what if we were? It's a free country.

True. But it's also getting late and we heard you from a block away.
Plus, did you say you were better than the Clash? Because I gotta tell you— "Rock the Casbah," "London Calling"... those are classics.
NJ POLICE
They're old! You're old!
Yo, bro. Chill.
Misfit
RAMONES
You two need to move along. Now!
Misfit
Fine! But we'll be back for the Battle of the Bands, which, by the way, we're totally going to win!
Those two boys in the Shakespeare show?
Good. They don't strike me as the Shakespeare types.
No way!
Sigh. Dad?
Yes?

They gave me a bigger part in the show today. I might need to rehearse more. But I promise—I'll keep my job on the boardwalk and can still help watch Emma.
You'll have to work harder and longer. At play practice, on the job, and at home.
Yes, sir. But acting in plays, being in shows—it's what I love more than anything in the world.
Good. Then at least that part won't feel like work, will it? What part did they give you in the play?
Puck.
Well, come on, Puck. Let's get you home. It sounds like you have a very busy day tomorrow.
Yes, that night I rode in the backseat of a police car for the first time.
To anyone who saw me, it looked like I'd just been arrested, when, in fact, I'd just been rescued.
A-113

A Midsummer Night's Dream
A Midsummer Night's Dream
Slurp Sip
Slurp Sip
The best part about being a theater nerd is that you always get to rehearsal a half-hour before everyone else.
Mmhmm. A famous poet once said: "Listen to silence. It has so much to say."
Jacky, I want to thank you for making sure Schuyler has some kids close to his age to hang out with over the summer.
Sluuurrrp!
Hoo-boy. Do I tell her what Schuyler tried to do at the taffy shop?

There are some things you may not know about my nephew.
Oh, good! She already knows Schuyler is a one hundred percent kleptomaniac. That makes things easier....
Slurrrp!
Schuyler's mother, my sister, died two years ago. His dad is still over in the Middle East, in Kuwait.
He's sweeping the desert for mines and unexploded bombs. It's slow, dangerous work, and it may not be finished until sometime next year.

Anyway, this school year, Schuyler lived outside Philadelphia with his grandparents on his dad's side. They're kind of old and kind of old-fashioned. They're also extremely strict.

Big-time. The authorities were about to ship him off to a juvenile detention facility. I went to Philly and promised everybody that I would take care of him this summer. That I'd supervise him and keep him out of trouble. So far, it's been working.
That's great.
So, thanks again, Jacky. You guys are helping Schuyler have the normal summer a teenage boy deserves. Especially one who's been through everything he has.
No problem!
If the authorities ever find out about Schuyler's attempted taffy snatching, they'll probably cart him off to that juvenile detention facility.
Hey, let's run a few lines.
Sounds good!

After our chat, I was determined to help Ms. O'Mara do everything she could to help Schuyler.
So, you wanted to introduce me to Jersey Shore food....
Yeah! It's the best.
Well, I wouldn't say it's the best. But it's what summer tastes like around here, so...
HOT DOGS
GYRO
TACO BURRITO
CORN DOGS SAUSAGES
Fried Dough
FRESH FUNNEL CAKES
PIZZA
NACHOS CHURROS
COTTON CANDY
POPCORN
Fresh Cut
Take your pick!

Hmm...
I've got an idea. Let's eat one of everything—starting with funnel cakes!
No, thanks. Been there, done that.
Barf!
Have the puke-stained T-shirt and ruined sombrero to prove it.
NY
Huh?
Long story.
Okay. So let's start with a sausage and pepper sandwich.
Ah, the king of Jersey Shore sandwiches. Good choice!
PIZZA
CHURROS
Fresh Cut
POPCORN
POPCORN
POPCORN

SIZZLE!
We'll take two, please.
CHOP!
This is fantastic!
Yup! Your stomach should start gurgling any second now.
I thought you didn't have any money?

H-h-hello, Jacky Ha-Ha-Hart. Your daddy and his po-po friends aren't here to protect you today?
I saw you pocket the change. Fork it over.
Not gonna happen.
Who the heck are you, dorkface?
Jacqueline Hart's theater colleague.
From that stupid Shakespeare show?
Indeed.
Poot!
Ew!
Ah, sausage sandwiches. Such delicious gas refineries. Or, as Sir William Shakespeare once said, "Blow, winds, and crack your cheeks."

Shakespeare made fart jokes?
Totally. Aunt Kathy's teaching me the best stuff.
Well, I don't care about Shakespeare or farts—
You should. I'm breaking some serious wind here.
Now, begone from here, you roguish knave! I desire that we be better strangers.
Thou art a boil upon mine buttocks!
Ha-ha-ha!
Were I like thee, I'd throw myself away!

KABOB
Thanks!
No problemo. That guy's a real dope.
I owe you one.
Sounds good. Invite me to your house for dinner. I'd like to say hello to your big sister.
Again.
Ha-ha-ha!

SALE!
Okay, okay. Come over to dinner tonight. We eat at six.
Cool. I'll be there.
Great. I'll tell Sophia.
Should I also tell her to wear a gas mask?
Nah. My tank should be empty by then!
NJ
Barber Shoppe

Schuyler's coming?
Here?
For dinner?
Schuyler?
Here? Dinner?
COOKIE
Hey! I'm on the phone over here! Go dunk your head in cold water or something!
I need to fix my hair!
Your hair looks fine—ugh, never mind.
Pizza will be here in a half hour or less, or it's free.

Did you know that Americans eat approximately one hundred acres of pizza a day? That's three-hundred-and-fifty slices per second. And pepperoni is America's favorite topping.
COOKIE
Actually, Emma, cheese isn't a topping.
No, it's not. It's cheese.
It's on top of the sauce, isn't it?
Never give up educating the masses, Victoria.
Sigh
Sometimes it seems like a fruitless struggle, Jacky.
Hey, maybe someday I could invite Jeff Cohen home for pizza.
Jeff and I are destined to be together, Jacky! We're like Shakespeare's Romeo and Juliet.
Without the dying stuff at the end, of course. And have you seen him in his cow costume? He makes for a very handsome heifer.

Do you think you could arrange a rendezvous?
What's a rendezvous?
It's French. For a meeting. Usually under the boardwalk.
I'll see what I can do, sis.
Thank you!
Oof!
DING DONG
He's here! Oh, my gosh! How do I look?
Like you just escaped a salon set up in a wind tunnel.
I mean that in a good way! You look beautiful.

Hey, Schuyler.
Hey, Jacky.
Sophia's in the kitchen.
Cool.
Hi, again, Sophia.
Hi.
Again.
I'm gonna go wait for the pizza.

A Walkman was sort of like an iPhone but without the phone or the apps—just the music. But the music was on a cassette tape.

How about music? Can you play music on your Walkman?
Like right now?
Sure, yeah. Go ahead.

We're dealing with a theft-and-shoplifting crime wave.
Really? Where?
Koko Puffs
Sweet Flakes
MILK
On the beach and the boardwalk. It's really snowballed in the last few days. If we don't put a stop to it soon, it could really hurt the tourist business.
That's horrible.
Look on the bright side, Father. If you're the police officer who cracks the case, you'll definitely be offered a full-time job in the fall.
Hmm. I guess you're right. I should go interview that angry professor again. Dig up some clues.
What angry professor?
He's from Princeton.
Does he know Sydney?
Didn't say.
NJ PD
He just yelled at us about his missing Walkman. Someone grabbed it off his towel when he went for a swim.
Wait, did Dad just say "Walkman"?

As in, Schuyler's Walkman?
No wonder he said it was a professor's Walkman.
Because he stole it from one!
BALLOON RACE
2 3 4 5
BALLOO
Hey, Jacky. I'm on my way to see Sophia, but she doesn't get her lunch break for another half hour.
Cool.
Cool as a cucumber. For a thief!
Yo, Jacky. Isn't it a little early to talk breaks? Or are you too busy with your new boyfriend to drum up some business over here?

He's not my boyfriend. He's my sister's.
Then what's he doin' here with you?
He can't hang out with my sister because she doesn't get her lunch break for another half hour.
Again with the break?
Sir? Would you like to take a break?
Me and the Pope. But we're both too busy.
How about I cover for you?
You suddenly a trained carnie?
No, sir. But I won a stuffed gorilla at the Frog Bog once.
Works for me.
$1 TO PLAY

The money box? Oooh, that might be a mistake....
Vinnie
I'm gonna get a Pepsi. Jacky's in charge.
PIZZA
Step right up, folks! Pop a balloon and take home a gorilla the size of a house.
Unless, of course, you're chicken. Bak-bak-baaak!

Don't stand too close to a bucket of KFC, buddy.
gissle
LLOO
PIZZA
Whoa! Look at this crowd. You and your new boyfriend done good!

Shakespeare was right when he wrote, "The course of true love never did run smooth."

Here you go!
Seems kinda light for a crowd this size.
Nobody paid with coins.
Well, I gotta book it. Sophia gets her break in five.
ER
RACE
CE
I wonder if he thinks Schuyler pocketed a few bucks.
PIZ
PSI
Wait. Do I think he took money?
I need to talk to Ms. O'Mara about this....

Acky!
Ate oop!
Midway Steak House
POP!
Can't let the kids see me without my head on. It's against every rule in the mascot handbook.
That must be a short read.

Is it true that you're dating Schuyler now?
I'm not dating anybody.
What about Bubblebutt?
His name is Bob. And I was just nice to him because he was nice to me.
Oh. So it's over?
It never started!
Good. Because you're breaking my dawg Bill's heart.
It's not intentional, Jeff. I like Bill.
Good. Because he told me to tell you that he likes you, too.
Okay, I'll talk to him.
Hey, Jeff? Can you bring your costume to rehearsal today? I know someone who loves seeing you wear it.
Is it your sister, Victoria? Because I love seeing her in her taffy uniform. It's so white and ruffly.
Well, she's working at the shop tonight—
Sweet! I can make a surprise guest appearance.
Thanks, Jacky! I've gotta bounce.

Hey, Jacky. Did you hear? Ronny got into Miss Saigon!
He's leaving the show!
On Broadway!
We need a new Tom Snout.
Any suggestions?
Schuyler in the show?
What about Schuyler?
If Schuyler's in the show, he'll be too busy to roam Seaside Heights on a crime spree.
Tom Snout could be a teenager.
And if he's funny....
Okay. Let's give him a try.

I'd be playing a wall?
Right. It's a joke. There are two lovers who have to talk through your fingers like it's a hole in the bricks.
Cool.
Schuyler played a scene with the adult actors, including Tony Keefer.
Tony used to star on the TV sitcom Who's in Charge?
His face was on the cover of TV Guide three different times.
TV GUIDE
TV GUIDE
KEEFE
TV GUIDE
TONY KEEFER
Guess who this is?
If you ever met him, he'd tell you. At least twice.

Schuyler handled his lines perfectly. He even earned some laughs.
You're good! You remind me of a young me.
Wow. My crazy idea might actually work!

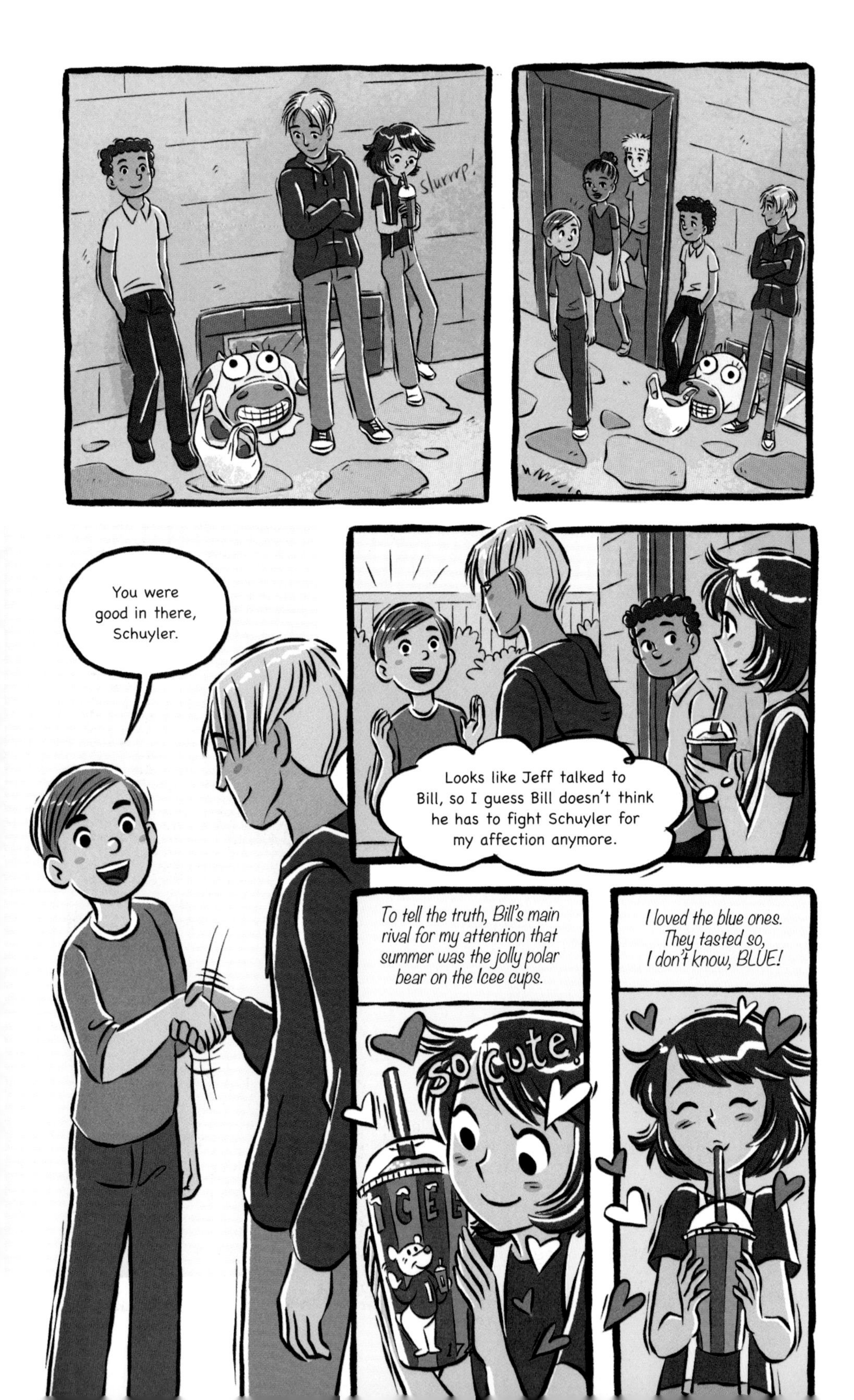
slurrrp!
You were good in there, Schuyler.
Looks like Jeff talked to Bill, so I guess Bill doesn't think he has to fight Schuyler for my affection anymore.
To tell the truth, Bill's main rival for my attention that summer was the jolly polar bear on the Icee cups.
so cute!
ICEE
I loved the blue ones. They tasted so, I don't know, BLUE!

Hey, Bill. Want to come over for dinner some night?
Sure! When's good?
After the show opens. We'll have pizza.
Cool.
The pizza invitation was my subtle way of telling him not to worry.
If I actually wanted a boyfriend, he'd probably be it. Why? Because he's the easiest guy to talk to that I've ever met.
But I'd been bitten by the acting bug. So my one true love that summer was the theater!
Hey, Jeff. Can I try on your cow costume?
I don't know. Bossy represents Swirl Tip Cones.
I won't do anything weird. I just want to try it on for a second.
But I'm supposed to meet Victoria later.
Just for one second. You won't be late for your date.

It's not a date. It's a prearranged coincidence.
I told Victoria I'd be stopping by the Taffy Shoppe after rehearsal.
Moo meyes. Ow oo I ook?
You look great.
Wow. You speak muffled cow better than anyone I know.
Heh. Yeah.
Okay, Schuyler. We need to go. Take off the costume.
Moh-kee.

TUG!
TWIST!
YANK!
Iss uck.
You snapped the latch? Oh man, I never snap the latch. It's rusty....
Om orry....
I need a screwdriver. Or a pair of pliers.

There's a toolbox downstairs.
Don't yank! I had to give Mr. Peterson a damage deposit. If you mess it up, I lose fifty bucks!
I'll be right back. And don't yank!
Did you hear that? Don't yank.
Yeh, I erd.
There you are!
Um, Victoria....
Taffe Shoppe

I couldn't wait for you a moment longer. Whenever I see you in that cow costume, I just want to jump over the moon! It even makes you look taller!
Oov ott de wong eye!
I don't understand what you said, but I want to learn the language!
I think you're simply bovine!
Eye ott cheff!
This is a case of mistaken identities to rival the ones in *A Midsummer Night's Dream*!

You know, I've never had a boyfriend before. I know we're not the same age...
...but I did some research, and did you know that male chimpanzees prefer older females? So this is scientifically okay....
Hey. I thought I'd stop by and see if...
FOOOMP!
Ahhhhh!
Pant
Pant
...Schuyler... was...
I thought you were Sophia's boyfriend!
I was!

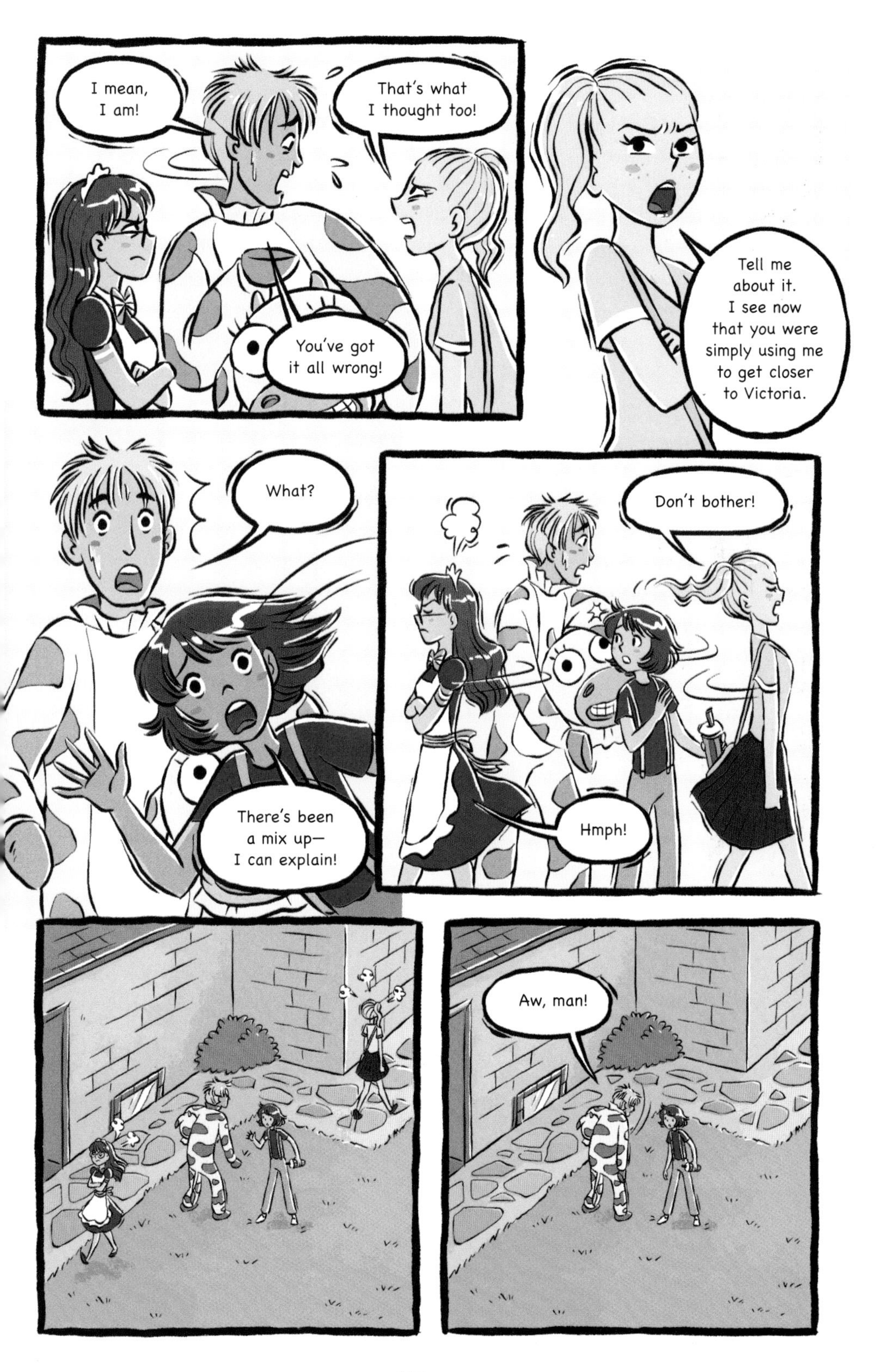
I mean,
I am!
That's what
I thought too!
You've got
it all wrong!
Tell me
about it.
I see now
that you were
simply using me
to get closer
to Victoria.
What?
There's been
a mix up—
I can explain!
Don't bother!
Hmph!
Aw, man!

I got home as fast as I could, hoping to mend fences. I didn't like having two broken hearts on the Jacky Ha-Ha scorecard.
Sounds like you really blew it, Jacky.
Victoria is in her room, reading a Jane Austen novel, hoping it will explain this romantic mess.
And do you know what Sophia is doing, Jacky?
Crying in her pillow?
Pfft. I wish! Well, not really.
She's on the phone with Mike Guadagno! My future boyfriend. The one who used to be her boyfriend!
So, thanks for nothing!
SOB!
Make that three broken hearts.

Guess she's mad at you now, too.
Yeah. Tonight's been my midsummer nightmare.
I heard. And you know what?
What?
I'm thinking I need a new role model.
If Jacky doesn't shape up, you'll definitely need a new role model, Riley.
Definitely.
Sydney! I thought you were still at Princeton.
I have a couple days off this week. So I thought I'd come home and spend them with you guys.
She missed the pizza.
SOB!
And, more importantly, I missed my sisters. Because family is more important than anything, Jacky.

Especially boys.
Things just got a little jumbled! I meant for Sophia to wind up with Schuyler and Victoria with Jeff.
Well, congratulations. Because they ended up here at home instead. Crying.
Heh-heh. In a way, the whole thing is semi-Shakespearean.
You know— summer love, mistaken identities....
The time is out of joint, O cursed spite, that ever you were born to set it right, Jacky.
That's not a direct quote, is it? I don't think any Shakespeare characters were ever named Jacky....
It's from *Hamlet.* Perhaps Shakespeare's best-known tragedy. And if you don't make things right for your sisters—and fast—that's exactly what this will turn into. A tragedy!

When Mom was over in Iraq, I used to write her letters all the time.
I found that telling her stuff was a lot easier when I wrote it down, instead of keeping it all locked up inside my head.
So that night, I decided to write a letter to Mom. For old times' sake.
And to ask her advice.
Dear Mom,
Things aren't going so great.
In fact, this is turning out to be the weirdest and worst summer of my young life, even though it should be one of the best

I mean, I have a big part in a big show.
I have a pretty fun job.
$1 TO PLA
Bill still has gorgeous hazel eyes and acts like he's crazy about me.
But that's the thing. I'm twelve. I think I want to go back to being eleven, when boys were just annoying creatures who picked boogers out of their noses.
I don't like feeling all giggly and goofy around boys. Well, actually, I do. And then I don't.
Have I mentioned that Bubblebutt has turned into Bob and he's not as bad as I thought he was during the first decade of my life?
He needs new friends besides Ringworm, but he's actually kind of sweet.

Maybe it's Shakespeare. But, all of a sudden, I'm running around Seaside Heights thinking about love, and when I'm not thinking about love, I'm playing matchmaker for other people to fall in love.

mike Guadagno

The problem is, my matchmaking is making everybody sad, when I just wanted to help them be happy.

And then there's Schuyler. He might be a thief. Or he might just really like taffy.

I know he likes Sophia, but do we, like, want her to be with a boy who might be a shoplifter?

I wonder what it was about Dad that made you fall in love with him, besides, of course, being the most handsome guy on the beach.

If you get a second, send me a reply.
You don't need to waste a stamp.
You can just slip it under my door. I'll probably be in my room. Crying.
Because I've messed up my summer and everybody else's.
Sincerely,
Your daughter Jacky

Mom

I never mailed that letter to my mother. Even though I didn't need a stamp.

That summer, she had enough problems without me giving her all of mine.

Mom

Two mornings later Sydney went back to Princeton...
POP!
...and I went back to work.
Physically, I was behind the counter at the Balloon Race booth.
Mike Guadagno
But mentally, all I could think was that I needed to make things right with my family and friends. To find a way to make them happy.
Because their unhappiness was all my fault.
And then it hit me. Ice cream.
No!
Frozen custard!!!

I told Bill about my plan to make things right, and he volunteered to help.
While I made arrangements at the Khor's Frozen Custard stand...
...Bill created invitations...
You're Invited 4 p.m. at Kohr's Frozen Custard!
...and secretly delivered them to Jeff,
Victoria,
Victoria
Schuyler,
Schuyler
and Sophia.
Sophia

KOHR'S
Thanks for letting us do this, Anne.
Of course! I love seeing a good comedy of errors get resolved.
They're here!
I hope this works.
Me too!
Victoria? Are you here for Schuyler?
Don't be immature, Jeff. Why would I be here for him? I'm here for you!
jingle jingle
Wait, why are you here, Schuyler? I thought you wanted to date Victoria.
What? No, I don't! I like you!
SQUEAL
SMOOCH!
I knew it!

Surprise!
Jacky? Did you arrange this delightful engagement?
Guilty! This is my way of saying I'm sorry for last night. Or, as Puck would put it: If Jacky Hart has offended, think but this, and all is mended— you did but slumber in the church parking lot, where I gave matchmaking a terrible shot. Give me your hands if we be friends. And now, Jacky Ha-Ha her paycheck amends.
CLAP
CLAP
CLAP
CLAP
CLAP
Kohr's Frozen Custard
That was the bomb, Jacky.
Let me pay you back for this. Aunt Kathy just—
No, that's okay. It's my treat.
We'll take that.

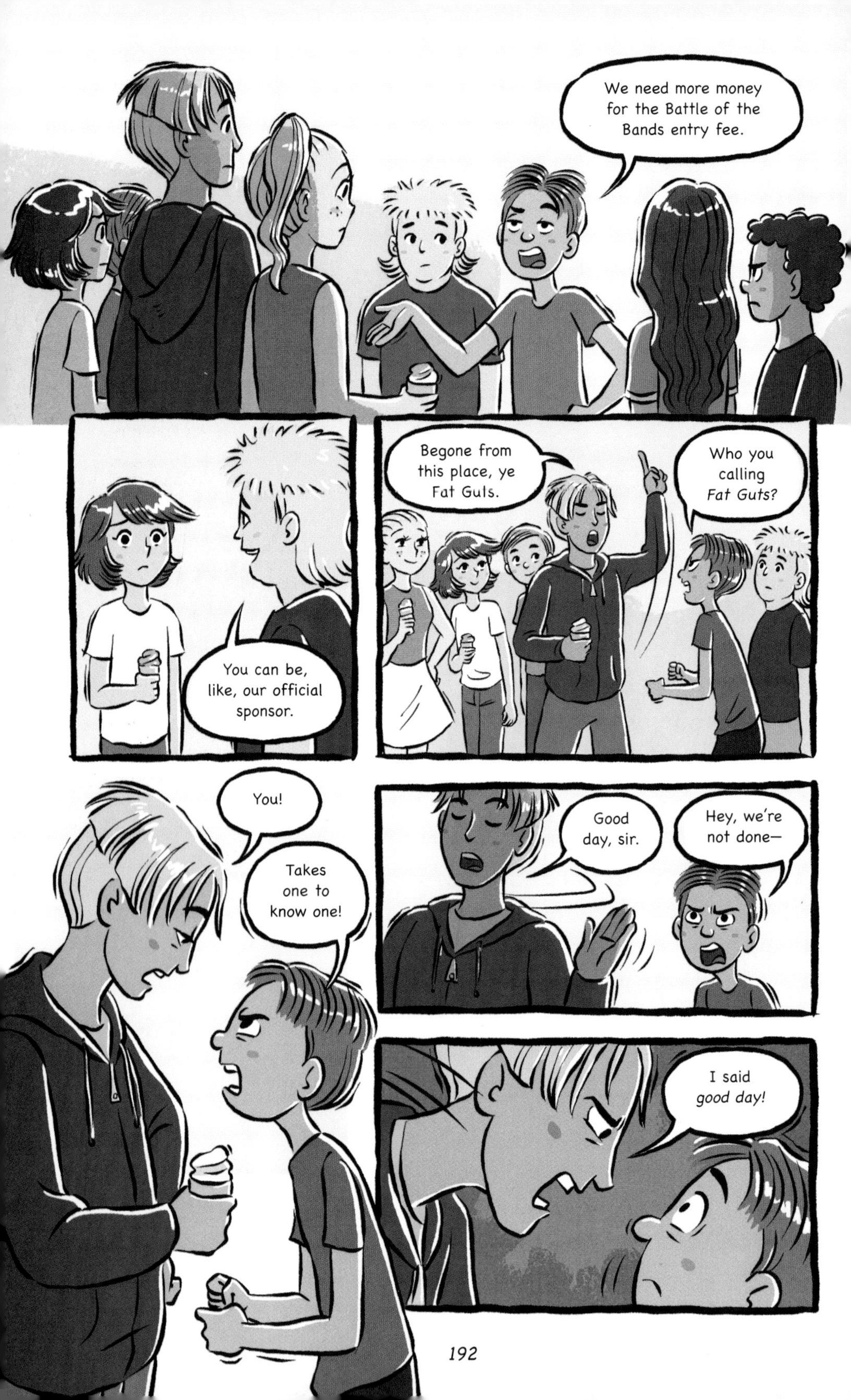
We need more money for the Battle of the Bands entry fee.
You can be, like, our official sponsor.
Begone from this place, ye Fat Guls.
Who you calling *Fat Guts*?
You!
Takes one to know one!
Good day, sir.
Hey, we're not done—
I said *good day!*

I'm sorry, Jacky.
He called us *Fat Guts!* Let's get him.
But—
Don't wimp out on me, Bubblebutt.
Yo. Who are you calling Bubblebutt?
You, Fat Guts!
You're a Fat Guts.
No, you are!
Nu-uh!
Yu-huh!
Nu-uh!
Yu-huh!
What a couple of dopes.

Later at rehearsal...
Sophia isn't off until later.
Well, Vinnie needs me for the late shift at the Balloon Race because he's taking a date to a movie. You can hang out there until then.
Cool.
RACE
Woohoo!
Pop that balloon!
Go! Go! Go!
Hey, is it okay for us to take this bill?
$1 TO PLAY

It's fine. Vinnie will sort it out with his bank.
THE UNITED STATES OF AMERICA
I532521190
FIVE
FIVE DOLLARS
Okay.
I can't believe how busy it is!
Vinnie's going to be super happy.
POP!
Looks like we got another winner!
$1 TO PLAY
Uh ee a ittle elp, acky. It's uck.
Can you watch the booth for a moment?
No problemo.
Come on. Head around back so no kids see you.

Wouldn't wanna to shatter the illusion.
Thanks, Jacky. I want Victoria to see the real me, not a cow.
Is she at the Taffy Shoppe tonight?
No. She's at home.
Oh. I guess I should learn her work schedule.
How about you come to dinner with me and Victoria and all our sisters one night?
For real?
Totally. We should probably wait until after the show opens, though.
You're the best, Jacky! Now I know why Bill is so crazy about you.

Are you in charge here? I'd like to play.
PLAY
Sure. Just one moment.
Sorry I had to take care of some stuff
Oh, no!

WATER BALLOON RACE
5
6
ACE
Yo, Jacky, you gotta check out this flick, *City Slickers*. It's about cows.
TO PLA
Yo, Jacky, where's the moola-boola?
Um...gone?
Whaddya mean, "gone"? Is that supposed to be some kind of joke?
I don't know what happened! But I can find out.
You better find out, or I'll make sure you end up in jail!
How much was in the box, Vinnie?
On a night like this? Fuhgeddaboudit. Had to be two, three hundred clams.
That's a lot of clams.

CREAM
What am I going to do?
What the heck is *Fat Guts?*
SHORE
FAT GUTS
Great. Now Schuyler is vandalizing property!
Phone
US Coins only
1 2 3
4 5 6

Ring! Ring!
Hello?
Where did you go?
Home. Aunt Kathy needed me to come home right away.
Someone stole all the money, Schuyler! Vinnie fired me....
I'm sorry, but I had to book. My dad was able to schedule a phone call from Kuwait, but he only had, like, fifteen minutes.
And you left the money box right there? In the booth?
Yeah. I tucked it under the counter and hid it on the shelf behind the Garfields.
Well, it was empty!
What?!
Look, where are you? We need to talk.
I'm on the boardwalk.
Stay there. I'm on my way. I can explain everything.
You better. Meet me at the cheese fry place.
US coins only

Cheese Fries
I didn't mean to bail on you like that, Jacky. But I would've missed talking to my dad.
But you left the booth without telling me. Was that on purpose?
I promise it wasn't.
But, hey, don't worry. Tomorrow I'll help you figure out who stole the money. We'll look for clues and junk, just like the detectives on *Law and Order*.
Sure. Let's play cops. I have nothing better to do until rehearsal. Did I mention—*I lost my job?*
Calm down, Jacky.
Telling me to calm down makes me less calm!
Sorry!
Everything's going to be okay. And since you're temporarily unemployed, tonight's cheese fries are on me.
TIPS

One cheese fries, please.
This is no good.
It's defaced. Also, Spock never had a goatee.
Where did you get that bill?
Actually, the evil Spock from the alternate universe in the first season episode *Mirror, Mirror* had a goatee.
Potato Wedges
Ahem. I've got five singles.
I'm sure you do. You're probably loaded. There were two or three hundred clams in that money box!

Not real clams. That would be gross.
Enjoy your cheese fries, Mr. Moneybags, because I'm not hungry.
And that's not real cheese, anyway. It's a liquid version of whatever kind of orange dust Cheetos is covered with.
Hey!
What, you think that five-dollar bill came from Vinnie's money box?
Well, duh. Where do you think it came from? The starship *Enterprise*?
Jacky! I can explain.
How about you pay first, kid? Then you can do all the explaining you want.
ieS 'n More
Sure. No problem.

Shakespeare said, "Lord, what fools these mortals be."
I was a fool to think Schuyler was a good guy. That he could ever become a good guy, given his sketchy past.
And I'm the biggest fool of them all!
I was especially foolish to let Sophia fall in love with him. And that's something I'm going to fix. Tonight!
Whatever. I like the bad ones. Johnny Depp is a bad boy on *21 Jump Street*. He broods. I like brooding.
He's a bad guy, Sophia.
Schuyler isn't bad that way. He's a criminal. A thief!

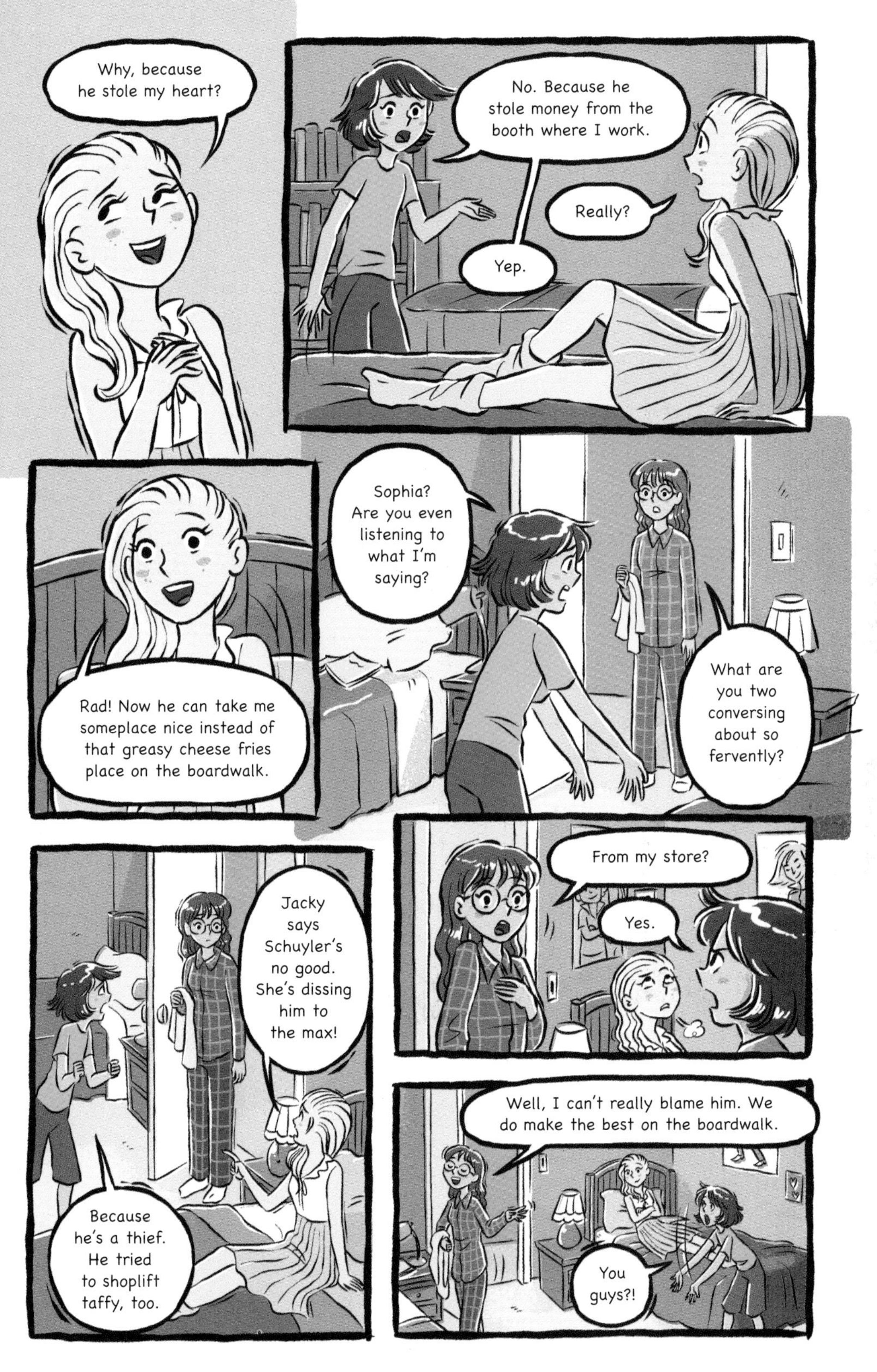
Why, because he stole my heart?
No. Because he stole money from the booth where I work.
Really?
Yep.
Rad! Now he can take me someplace nice instead of that greasy cheese fries place on the boardwalk.
Sophia? Are you even listening to what I'm saying?
What are you two conversing about so fervently?
Jacky says Schuyler's no good. She's dissing him to the max!
Because he's a thief. He tried to shoplift taffy, too.
From my store?
Yes.
Well, I can't really blame him. We do make the best on the boardwalk.
You guys?!

It's a little late for shouting, girls.
Dad, we need to talk about something serious.
Jacky? Please. If you believe in the power of love...don't!
Is this about Mike Guadagno?
It better not be!
It's about Schuyler!
Oh. Okay.
Who the heck is Schuyler?
Ms. O'Mara's nephew. He's your thief, Dad. He's the one who stole the Princeton professor's Walkman. The one who spray-painted that Fat Guts graffiti on the rolled-down gate. The one who just robbed the booth where I work and got me fired!
He also tried to shoplift some taffy. But it's so delicious, you can't really call that a crime, can you, Dad?
Yes, dear. I can. I'm a cop.
Let's go to the kitchen.

This kid Schuyler, Ms. O'Mara's nephew, has been in all sorts of trouble with the police in Philly. He came here this summer to clean up his act; otherwise, I'm pretty sure he was headed for the state penitentiary.
The penitentiary?
Well, maybe juvie. Is that what they call a prison for kids?
Only in the movies.
Oh.
Well, anyway, Schuyler came here, but he didn't clean up his act. I saw him trying to shoplift at Victoria's store.
Did he steal anything?
No. He saw me watching him before he could. He put the candy back in the bin.

But the other night, he was showing off a Sony Walkman. Said it was the kind college professors use. The kind he probably snatched off the beach.
And that graffiti on the rolled-down security gate that said *Fat Guts?* That's from a Shakespearean insult. Schuyler's big on those. He's memorized a ton.
Anything else?
Yes. He cost me my job by stealing from the money box.
How do you know he was the one who stole it?
Easy. Some college kids gave us a five-dollar bill that had been defaced with a rubber stamp to turn Abraham Lincoln into Mr. Spock from *Star Trek*.
Really?
Yup. Later, when Schuyler was trying to buy my silence with an order of cheese fries, he paid with the exact same five-dollar bill!
COOK

If you arrest Schuyler, get him to confess, and give Vinnie back the money he stole, maybe Vinnie will give me back my job, because I kn-kn-know how important it is that we all w-w-work this summer and I'm s-s-so s-s-sorry I lost my job.
Everything's going to be okay, Jacky.
I'm going to call this in.
Where can we find this boy Schuyler?
sob At M-M-Ms. O'Mara's apartment. She has a place over on B-B-Bay Terrace.

Thank you, Jacky. I think we have all we need.
Jacky! What'd you tell these guys?
The truth.
But I didn't do anything wrong!

Tell it to the detective.
You want to sit in on this, Mac?
Yes, sir.
Wait for me out front.
Yes, sir.
For the first time since we met all those months ago in the detention hall, Ms. O'Mara wasn't exactly thrilled to see me.
WE CARE!
FBI
Maybe a line from our show will break the ice.

WE CARE!
FBI
Ill met by moonlight, proud Titania.
There's no moonlight, Jacky. The clouds blocked it all out tonight. The same way they blocked your brain, apparently.
What were you thinking?
That Schuyler needs to give my boss back his money.
He didn't take it.
Oh, really? Then why did he have that Mr. Spock five-dollar bill?
You mean like this one?
Or this one?
Wh-wh-where....
At the grocery store. And the gas station.

This one came from Latoya Sherron because I lent her five bucks last week. These are all over Seaside Heights. So when the police are done interrogating Schuyler, they can come after me and Latoya.
Wh-wh-what about the W-W-Walkman?
Mine. I let him borrow it.
Maybe, Jacky, you need to slow down. Give your mouth a chance to catch up with your brain.
Okay. Well, wh-wh-what about the g-g-graffiti?
RIINNNGGG!
Seaside Heights Police ...Yes, ma'am... On your wall? Red spray paint? And you saw the perpetrator? Which way did he run? Okay, I'm sending out a car....
No, ma'am, I don't think the boy means anything personal by it. *Fat Guts* is just what this kid tags every time he grabs a can of red spray paint.
Schuyler wasn't a criminal. He was just a high-school kid who couldn't catch a break.

Especially that summer, when I made the biggest mistake of my life.
CARE
I made the police arrest an innocent kid.
POLICE
NEW JERSEY POLICE
You should go home. I need to stay here and see if I can repair the damage.
Okay. I'm sorry, Dad.
We put an innocent boy in handcuffs, Jacky. We dragged him out of bed and hauled him into the station!
Sorry seems inadequate.
This whole incident isn't going to look particularly great on Dad's application for a permanent gig on the force.
Experience: Writing up parking tickets and arresting the wrong children at 2 a.m.

Sigh
Why so g-g-glum, Jacky Ha-Ha?
Ugh, what are you doing here?
I'm celebrating. Haven't you heard the news?
Check it out. We scored the entry fee for Battle of the Bands. In fact, it's more than we need. Toxic Trash is going to play and win that prize money!

We're going to be rock stars and ain't nobody ever gonna call me Fat Guts again like your dipstick boyfriend.
He's not my boyfriend.
I just happened to see him riding in the back of a police car. I hope he's all right!
What'd he get busted for, huh? Graffiti? Stealing? Ha-ha! What a loser!
You seem to know a lot about the trouble Schuyler got in.
Come on, Jacky. I'm on my way to Bob's house. Come celebrate with us. It's par-tay time!
We can pick up some cheese fries on the way.
Where? Everything on the boardwalk is closed. It's three o'clock in the morning.
TACOS
BURGER
Burritos Fajitas
Fries Shake
Too true. So celebrate tomorrow, Jacky Ha-Ha.

No thanks. I like to not throw up my food.
Buy yourself the j-j-jumbo box with extra ch-ch-cheese and think about m-m-me.
Oh, come on. I insist. I can afford it.
Fine. If it means you'll go away and leave me alone.
We'll see if that's what you want once I'm a rock star.
THE UNITED STATES OF AMERICA
FIVE
FIVE DOLLARS

Knock
Knock
Hey, Jacky. What do you want to arrest me for today?
Nothing. But if you want, you can lock me up for being an idiot.
Seriously, Schuyler. I'm so sorry.
Really?
Yes.
Prove it.
How?
Step in and enjoy some of my aunt's delicious pancakes.
Um, isn't Ms. O'Mara a terrible cook?
The worst.

Are these things even cooked?
Mmmmm. Good pancakes, Ms. O'Mara.
Thank you, Jacky.
PANCAKE mix
Golden Syrup
So, you said you have something to tell us.

First, I want to say again how sorry I am. I really mean it. And I think I know who's responsible for all the thefts and stuff. Bubblebutt and Ringworm. I think they did it to raise money for their Battle of the Bands entry fee.
And I'm pretty sure that Ringworm picked up on Schuyler's *Fat Guts* Shakespearean insult and started to graffiti it around town to help me frame the wrong guy.
Putting the suspicion on Schuyler was Ringworm's plan all along. And I fell for it hook, line, and sinker.
Last night he gave me this from a wad of cash in his pocket. And he had red paint on his hands and jeans.
The problem is that it's all circumstantial evidence. What if I'm wrong? I can't go to my Dad now that I've screwed up so bad by blaming Schuyler. It'd be way better if they'd just, you know, confess.

The play's the thing
Wherein I'll catch the conscience of the king!
Um, we're talking about Bubblebutt and Ringworm.
Not Elvis Presley.
It's a line from *Hamlet*. He adds a few details to a play that a troupe of traveling actors is going to perform for the king, so the king will react badly and confess to killing Hamlet's father.
Does it work?
Yes. Just like a mousetrap.
Wait, I think I might have an idea....

The next day before our dress rehearsal, we got together and I told them about my mousetrap idea.
The Battle of the Bands?
Exactly. We need this to be public. It's no good unless we expose them in front of everyone.
Slight problem. None of us plays the guitar.
Or the drums.
Or anything.
I play the tuba.
Some.
Dude. Nobody wants to hear a tuba at a rock concert.
We don't need instruments.
Uh, yes we do. It's a *battle of bands*....
And we'll be a band of merry players!
Who don't play music?
Exactly. Come on, you guys! What's Shakespeare but old-fashioned rhyming rap with a hip-hop beat?

I can scratch out a beat on a turntable.
I can make bass noises with my mouth.
PFFF-BBBBBT-BTH-BBBBBT-PTHTTTHHHH
That was actually pretty good.
Told ya!
We could write up some fun lyrics about a group called Toxic Sludge, which everyone will know is really Toxic Trash.
We can have them bragging about stealing Sony Walkmans from professors. Robbing money boxes on the boardwalk. Spraying graffiti in drippy red paint.
If we do it right, those guys will freak out!
Wait a second. Those guys had to rob, cheat, and steal to raise the entry fee. How are we going to come up with five hundred bucks?
I can help with that.

Kathy told us what's going on, so we've been listening in. I love your diabolically clever scheme. Kindly allow me to pay for your mousetrap. I'm a millionaire, after all!
And since I'm one of the official judges for the contest, I don't think you kids will have any trouble winding up in the show. But you'll need an act and a name for your group.
We've got both!
Introducing, the Band of Bards!
We're the Toxic Sludge, We'll steal all your fudge,
You want some graffiti? Try *Fat Guts*, sweetie!
Grab your cassette player, forsooth!
We'll steal money right out of your booth!
Clap clap clap clap Ha-ha-ha
I'll admit that our lyrics need some work.

We kept rehearsing our Battle of the Bands number after every Midsummer Night's Dream rehearsal.
We only had a week to work out our routine, complete with break-dance moves.
Jeff and I worked on the lyrics for our Toxic Sludge number.
Meredith found some backing samples to scratch out on a turntable.
SKRRRR-TCH-SKRRRTCH
VVVP-VVVP-VVVVVVP
And Bill turned his mouth into a beatbox.
BBBBBT-BTH-BBBBBT-PTHTTTHHH

Finally, the night arrived.
Battle of the Bands
I'm sorry Jacky said all those mean and horrible things about you.
Me too. But she and I are cool now.
What about us?
Oh, we're super cool.
Good.

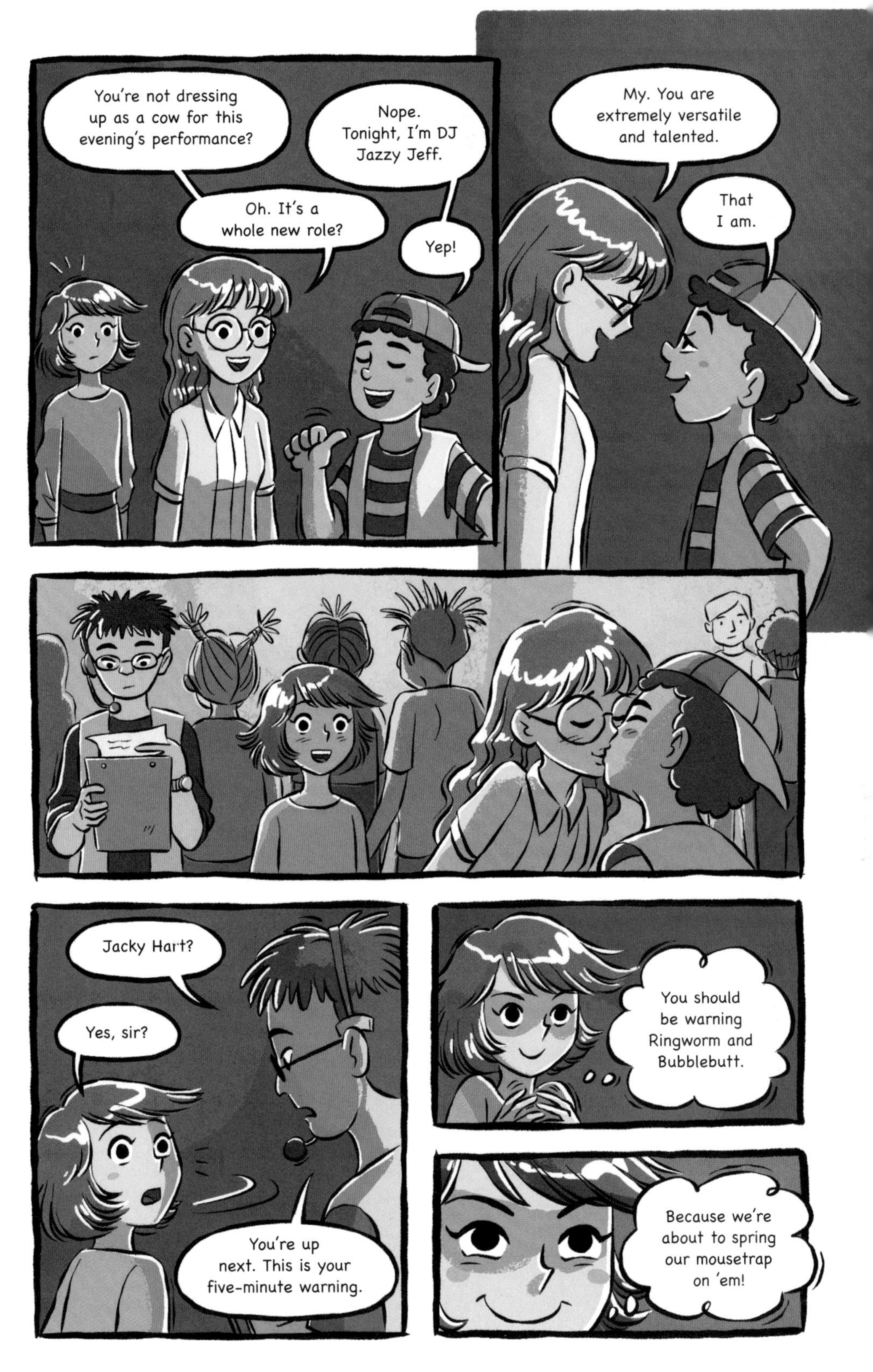
You're not dressing up as a cow for this evening's performance?
Nope. Tonight, I'm DJ Jazzy Jeff.
Oh. It's a whole new role?
Yep!
My. You are extremely versatile and talented.
That I am.
Jacky Hart?
Yes, sir?
You're up next. This is your five-minute warning.
You should be warning Ringworm and Bubblebutt.
Because we're about to spring our mousetrap on 'em!

CREW
Toxic Trash
Huh. Has there been a switch in their rankings? Bob used to call the shots.
Now it seems that Ringworm is bullying *him*.
The bully has become the bullied.
What are you doing here, Jacky Ha-Ha?
And how come you're not in jail, Skee-Ball? Everybody knows you're the one who spray-painted that *Fat Guts* graffiti up and down the boardwalk.

You mean that's what you want everybody to think. But you did it, didn't you?
Ha! I didn't do nothing.
Which means you did something.
Huh?
It's called grammar, dingus. Study it sometime!
Battle of the Bands
And now, ladies and gentlemen, please welcome our next group, representing Shakespeare Down the Shore, here they are, one of Latoya Sherron's personal faves—the Band of Bards!
Pay close attention to the lyrics. I think you'll enjoy them.

This one goes out to Shakespeare, who wrote: "Honesty is the best policy. If I lose mine honor, I lose myself."
We are the thieves from Toxic Sludge! We'd be in jail if we met a judge!
BBBT-BTH
BBBT
We stole a Walkman on the beach, Robbed any money box we could reach!
We sprayed graffiti, laughed off our bubble butts.
TOXIC

Did it up in red, yo.
We're ye old Fat Guts!
You heard it right,
on this stage tonight.
RRR-TCH
KRTCH
VVVP
We sprayed graffiti, laughed off our bubble butts.
Did it up in red, yo. We're ye old Fat Guts!
And though this might make you squirm,
But you can call me Ringworm!
Woohooo!!!!
Encore!
Yeah!
Band of Bards! Band of Bards!
Toxic Trash

Did you enjoy that?

Yeah. That was super cute. You looked like a bunch of ballerinas out there. But you know what, Sky-dork? You're going to enjoy our song even better.

What? You're doing a solo act? 'Cause it looks like your partner in crime abandoned you.

You mean Bubblebutt? No problem. I've got an understudy for that big chicken.

I think you nerds know my big brother, the high school superstar Travis Wormowitz.

The one you jerks got kicked out of the Shakespeare show.

Travis is your b-brother?

Duh. How do you think I got my nickname? I'm Reggie Wormowitz. Bob turned it into Ringworm. So I turned him into Bubblebutt. Fair is fair, after all.

Schuyler the liar. The thieving highflier. The sneaky, crooked smiler.
Toxic Trash
They even had a verse about Schuyler being arrested and sent to prison, which wasn't true.
But the audience didn't know that.
Bands
That's right. Toxic Trash had the same plan that we did, before we even came up with our plan.
Guess they had the same rhyming dictionary we did.
Our lyrics were better, man.
Our music was better, too.
We didn't enter the Battle of the Bands to win. We did it to clear Schuyler's name and to get Ringworm to confess.
Gee, Jacky. That sure worked out well, didn't it?

I guess I won't be recording Ringworm's confession after all.
CLICK
This isn't over!
You're right. Sounds like they've got a third verse....
PROPS

I need this to record something.
What do you want to record? All those horrible things Toxic Trash are saying about me because you used to believe it, too?
Look, I'm sorry. Getting you arrested was the biggest mistake I've ever made in my life. But this is no time for whining.
Up, and away
Our soldiers stand full fairly for the day!
Huh?
It's Shakespeare. What? Do you think you're the only one who can memorize obscure quotes?
Now disappear, you guys. It's time for Jacky Ha-Ha to get into character.
Who are you going to be?

I'm, like, Toxic Trash's number one fan? Seriously, dudes. I am!
We're Toxic Trash!
Toxic Trash
We were totally awesome!
I'm always awesome.
EXIT
Guess those middle school dweebs couldn't stand the heat.
We showed them!
Toxic Trash
It was time for the performance of my life: pretending I loved Toxic Trash and doing it without the Wormowitz brothers figuring out who I was!
Wow! That was so great!
Click
Walkman

I'm Brianna from Long Beach Island, and I am in looooove with your music. You guys, like, rock!
Chya! Totally!
Thanks. I usually perform in nonmusical shows. But I was glad I was able to demonstrate my range as a performer. I'm quite good, aren't I?
The best!
They don't recognize me! This might actually work!
You looked so mean and nasty out there! I like bad boys.
You want bad? I'll give you bad.
Please! Tell me everything. And is it okay if I record you? Because, well, I'd totally like to fall asleep every night with your voices in my headphones.
No problemo. Me and my lame ex-friend, Bob? We tore up Seaside Heights this summer.
I bet if the world knew that, they'd never call you Ringworm again.

They better not! My name is Reggie. Reggie Wormowitz.

And I'm his big brother, Travis. The guy who should be starring as Puck in Shakespeare Down the Shore this summer. But the casting system was rigged. Sad.

Bob and I robbed, like, a half dozen game booths, man. Stole all the cash out of this one balloon-pop stand where that clown Schuyler was supposed to be standing guard.

Totally framed him.

Which was doubly sweet, because the chick who worked there stole my part in *A Midsummer Night's Dream*. And they got her fired!

I also stole a Walkman from this one dorky dude's beach bag. And did graffiti, too. Because I didn't like that dude Schuyler calling me *Fat Guts*.

So you made it look like he did it? That is so clever!
Yeah. He even got arrested for it. And, to seal the deal, Travis and I wrote that song you just heard about him.
Will that be on your first album?
Totally!
Toxic Trash
They told me everything. Which also meant they told the Walkman everything.
So I had their full confession on tape. And since they gave me permission to record them, it made it admissible as evidence.
Yeah. The Harts watched a lot of cop shows on TV.
Toxic

The next morning, I tailed Dad and his Seaside Heights PD patrol car.
POLICE

Why didn't I just immediately hand over my tape-recorded confessions?
POLICE
POLICE

Well, I was a little like the girl who cried wolf. My "evidence" misled Dad once. It'd be better, I figured, if he discovered the tape on his own.
STOP
POLICE
DD
DD
POLICE

I wanted Dad to be the one to discover the evidence that would bring the summertime crime spree to a stop.
POLICE
I figured it might help him land the full-time gig after Labor Day.
And help him forget (or at least forgive) my jumbo-sized mistake.

Nine days later, the Shakespeare Down the Shore production of A Midsummer Night's Dream had its opening performance.
That was my professional debut.
The show was fantastic! I didn't stutter or miss a single line.
Being on that stage with a cast of professional actors made me realize that if I could perform for a living—if I could become a professional, too—I would never have to work a day in my life.
So, good night unto you all.
Give me your hands, if we be friends,
And Robin shall restore amends.

Wow.
Yeah.
Did all that stuff really happen, Dad?
Just as your mother tells it.
Yes, girls, that was the summer a lot of dreams came true. And not just for me.
Your grandfather landed his first official cop job.
Congratulations Students!
Your grandmother graduated first in class from cop school.
5 6
$1
Vinnie got most of his money back. I got my job back, and it was excellent practice for my future career in show biz.

It was also the summer when I quit calling Bob Brownkowsi Bubblebutt.
Because he kept trying to become the very decent human being he is today.
BOB
The summer of 1991 was also famous for your aunt Victoria meeting your uncle Jeff.
Not to mention your aunt Sophia meeting your uncle Schuyler.
I know we all keep him in our prayers as he performs the same duties today that his father performed in the First Gulf War. He makes us all very proud.

Well, girls, I have a big day tomorrow. And I still have to get over my first-day jitters! But I want to leave you with words better than I could ever write. The ones Mr. Shakespeare wrote in *All's Well That Ends Well*. I repeat them to myself on a daily basis, and I even have them framed so they can travel with me wherever I go.
Love all, trust a few
Do wrong to none.
If you do that, my darling Grace and Tina, trust me: You'll be howling at the moon with joy on a regular basis.
Goodnight, Mom! We love you, and break a leg!
Good night, my loves, and I'll see you in a few weeks.
"Love all, trust a few
Do wrong to none."

Jady
This one's for you, Shakespeare.

AAAAA-WOOOOOOOOOOOOOOOOO!!!!

ABOUT THE AUTHORS

JAMES PATTERSON received the Literarian Award for Outstanding Service to the American Literary Community from the National Book Foundation. He holds the Guinness World Record for the most #1 *New York Times* bestsellers, including *Max Einstein, Middle School, I Funny,* and *Jacky Ha-Ha*, and his books have sold more than 385 million copies worldwide. A tireless champion of the power of books and reading, Patterson created a children's book imprint, JIMMY Patterson, whose mission is simple: "We want every kid who finishes a JIMMY Book to say, 'PLEASE GIVE ME ANOTHER BOOK.'" He has donated more than three million books to students and soldiers and funds over four hundred Teacher and Writer Education Scholarships at twenty-one colleges and universities. He has also donated millions of dollars to independent bookstores and school libraries. Patterson invests proceeds from the sales of JIMMY Patterson Books in pro-reading initiatives.

CHRIS GRABENSTEIN is a *New York Times* bestselling author who has collaborated with James Patterson on the Max Einstein, I Funny, Jacky Ha-Ha, Treasure Hunters, and House of Robots series, as well as *Word of Mouse, Katt vs. Dogg, Pottymouth and Stoopid, Laugh Out Loud*, and *Daniel X: Armageddon*. He lives in New York City.

ADAM RAU was born in Minnesota and moved to New York to attend The School of Visual Arts. In 2004 he landed a job in children's publishing, and before long was acquiring and editing graphic novels for young readers, which he has been doing for over ten years. Adam lives in Jersey City with his wife and dog.

BETTY C. TANG has been in the animation and illustration world for more than 25 years. She has worked for acclaimed studios including DreamWorks Animation and Disney Television Animation, co-directed the Chinese animated feature film *Where's the Dragon?*, and illustrated for books and magazines. Born in Taiwan, she now lives in Los Angeles, California, and writes and illustrates for children.